SCARRED KNUCKLES 2

ASSA RAYMOND BAKER

GOOD 2 GO PUBLISHING

SCARRED KNUCKLES 2
Written by Assa Raymond Baker
Cover Design: Davida Baldwin, Odd Ball Designs
Typesetter: Mychea
ISBN: 978-1-947340-52-7
Copyright © 2020 Good2Go Publishing
Published 2020 by Good2Go Publishing
7311 W. Glass Lane • Laveen, AZ 85339
www.good2gopublishing.com
https://twitter.com/good2gobooks
G2G@good2gopublishing.com
www.facebook.com/good2gopublishing
www.instagram.com/good2gopublishing

PREFACE

Racine County Jail did not have Beysik's release paperwork processed until just before midnight. Beysik was lucky to find someone to accept twenty dollars to give him a ride to the gas station where his car was left parked when he was arrested earlier that evening. Mercy Bondz was forever inclined to suspect the police of doing sneaky things to try to entrap him. This memory of his dad popped into his mind when he made it back to his car. So Beysik instantaneously removed the battery from his cell phone when he opened the clear plastic bag containing his personal property that had been taken from him upon his arrest. He made plans to buy a new phone as soon as the store opened. But until then, Beysik decided to use his tablet to communicate with his girl, Nyte, and the rest of his team via social media.

There was no doubt that Beysik Bondz was his father's son. Through and through, Beysik did his best to be an emotionally in control individual. But it was hard to be, with all of the craziness that had been happening in his world over the past few weeks. First, there was the mess with his guys being killed inside the Racine brothel because of the two young runaways his dad had sent down to him to put to work.

Now a detective came all the way from Milwaukee just to tell him about his parents' murders. He did not know what to do. He dialed both of his parents' numbers, hoping the detective was just trying to trick him into telling her something about his father. He then tried to reach Noeekwol, whose phone also went straight to voicemail. Beysik then decided just to head to his parents' house to see what was going on for himself. If it was all bad, just like the detective had said, he hoped to find his big brother there, so they could decide where to go from there together.

* * *

The harmonic tintinnabulation of Tabitha's phone was annoying. Her soon to be ex-partner, Sadd, had gotten in touch with the Federal agent that was heading the investigation of the deceased human trafficker, Mercy Bondz. Sadd easily convinced the gung-ho Fed to join in on the arrest operation to take down who Sadd believed to be the new head of the city's deadly trafficking ring. The phone continued to ring. In a confused fog, Tabitha let it go to voicemail; but as soon as the loud ringing stopped, Sadd called back again.

"What?" she mumbled in a sleepy voice.

"Allison, I got sight on B. Bondz entering the south side residence of his parents, and I thought you might wanna be here when we go in and arrest that asshole!" Detective Sadd said excitedly.

"Wait! Where are you and who are you with?" she inquired, dragging herself upright in bed. Tabitha instantly noticed that Bret had not come home yet.

"Wake the fuck up! I said I'm outside of Mercy Bondz's residence. I got the Feds to let us team up with them on their surveillance of the place. Do you want to be here when we go in, or not?" he repeated with a slight attitude.

"Yeah. Don't do anything until I get there," she answered, jumping out of her warm lonely bed and rushing into the bathroom to relieve her bladder of the half bottle of Barefoot wine that she drank in anger when she got home from work.

"I thought you might. So I already sent a car to pick you up. It should be there shortly. Allison, if you're not ready when the car gets there, I'm going ahead without you," he informed her before he then ended the call without another word.

Tabitha hurriedly got herself together. She pulled her long strawberry blonde tresses back into a loose French braid, and then wrestled on some black fitted jeans and slipped into a pair of black Nike Air Force Ones and a long sleeved dark blue U.W. Madison T-shirt. She then grabbed her badge and gun on the way out to an unmarked black Ford SUV that was waiting for her out front of her house.

Tabitha introduced herself to the Federal agent behind the wheel once she was seated inside. Then the agent rushed the detective to meet up with her partner with lights flashing. Once there, the SWAT team that was assembled up the street from the Bondz family home readied themselves for the raid.

"Sadd!" Tabitha exclaimed to get her partner's attention while she walked toward him, standing with a small group of police dressed in full riot gear.

"I'm glad you showed up. We are about to storm the place."

"With the Feds?" she asked in a surprised hushed voice.

"Yeah, but we have point on this. All they're interested in is the pimp's personal records of his human trafficking operation. B. Bondz is all ours," he explained joyously.

"Sadd, just for the record, I still don't believe Beysik Bondz had any part in the murders of his parents. With that wise ass lawyer that his family has on call, it tells me that this isn't going to end well for us," she said, strapping on her Kevlar police vest.

"I'll be sure to note that in my shift report. Now let's go!"

It was approximately 2:25 a.m. when Detective Sadd gave the order to the tactical officers surrounding the house to move in. Two officers ran up the front porch steps with a black, heavy, steel battering ram, and waited until both detectives were in position behind them. They then promptly busted down the door.

* * *

Beysik had drunk himself to sleep when he made it to his parents' house, so he was on the sofa when the sudden loud boom snapped him awake. All he saw were darkly dressed men with assault rifles and riot pumps rush his way. On pure survival instinct and the thought of his murdered parents, Beysik scrambled off the sofa and made a dash toward the dining room table. He had left his gun there when he arrived and found the place calm.

Detective Sadd first spotted Beysik's frantic scamper and quickly turned his weapon on him.

"Hey, don't move another step! Get down now!" he barked.

Still a little drunk, Beysik made a sudden turn toward the sound of the unfamiliar male voice in the darkness of the house. That's when the detective saw the silhouette of something he believed was a weapon in Beysik's hand and fired four rapid yet accurate shots into his torso. At that very same moment, Noeekwol came rushing from the bedroom. He was unarmed but ready to defend himself and Heaven from whomever was behind the commotion.

"Police! Get down! Get down now, and place your hands at your side so I can see them!" Tabitha yelled with her gun trained on him.

"Wait! What the fuck is this about?" Noeekwol demanded, complying with the detective's orders.

He then saw his little brother laid out in the middle of the floor, fighting to hold onto his life.

"What in the hell did y'all do that for? Beysik! Bey! Beysik, hold on, bro! Hey, one of y'all go get him some help! Do something! Help him!"

Noeekwol begged the SWAT officers that were just standing around.

He was unable to get back up because three officers had quickly pounced on his back.

Tabitha made her way over to her partner, who was now standing over Beysik looking a bit distraught.

"Sadd, what's wrong?" she inquired as she followed his stare and saw that Beysik was holding a TV remote control. He was still clutching it while fighting for his life.

"I thought he was about to fire on us. I didn't see what he was holding," Sadd said while looking at her. "Allison, you saw what he did, didn't you? Please tell me you saw what I did?" he pleaded in a shaky hushed voice.

Tabitha said nothing. She only rushed to Beysik's side to try to slow the bleeding until the EMTs were allowed inside of the house. Two medics rushed in and went right to work on getting the wounded man stabilized to transport him to the hospital.

As they worked on him, the SWAT officers zip tied Noeekwol's hands and then stood him up. Noeekwol heard Detective Sadd tell another officer that they should just let Beysik die. In the champ's extreme agitation, he broke free of the plastic cuffs and charged at Sadd. Noeekwol slugged him with his signature hard, heavy, non-stop violent combination of fists, knees, and elbows.

The shocked officers closest to the detective paused a moment and then snapped into action, tasing Noeekwol twice before he dropped to the floor. By that time, Sadd was bloody and unconscious. The FBI agents placed steel cuffs on Noeekwol this time and quickly dragged him out of the house.

All Heaven could do was watch helplessly as Beysik was put in the back of an ambulance and raced away, while Noeekwol was locked in the back of a black and white squad car that raced away in a different direction.

ONE

WALKING THROUGH THE HALLS of his new maximum security home, Noeekwol Bondz tried not to stare as he scanned the faces of the other men he passed on the way to the security director's office. This was his second trip there that day.

"Heyyyy, Bucky," a three hundred pound plus bad ass biker looking inmate with a bold White Pride tattoo covering the right side of his ugly face, disrespectfully greeted the champ's transport officer. "I see you got me some fresh meat!" he growled, before blowing a kiss at Noeekwol.

"Oooooh, guess who I'm fucking tonight," the biker's bald red bearded friend teasingly exclaimed, winking at the champ.

"Yeah, yeah! Just keep it moving, gentlemen!" Buckley ordered them after correcting them on the mispronunciation of his name.

"Fuck that! I bet that coco boy likes it rough. Don't you, boys?" the big man asked, laughing loudly with his two buddies as they kept it moving on down the main corridor.

"Bondz, don't pay them knuckleheads no mind. They talk crap like that to all the newcomers they see," Officer Buckley explained while they waited for the security door to be opened for them.

"I ain't worried about 'em."

Noeekwol looked at the faces of all of the other inmates who passed him and Buckley in the corridor. Many of them wore hard scowls, but the fear in their eyes exposed their truths. Others' eyes were cold and dark, and they did not match the bright smiles on the men's faces. The champ knew that those were the ones he really needed to watch out for. Being a cage fighter, Noeekwol had seen that crazed gaze many times just before his opponent tried to knock his head off for the fun of it.

"I know you're not. I bet you could take 'em all at once, can't you?" Buckley inquired right when the lock buzzed for them to enter into the main office.

"I didn't get to be the light heavyweight champ by doubting myself. When I'm faced with a fight, my only objective is to win, whether it be by knockout or tapout, as long as at the end I'm not the one who is being carried out," he answered boastfully as Officer Buckley pushed open the heavy steel door and then escorted him through.

"Wait here! Let me see if she's ready for you," Buckley said before going over and knocking on the director's door.

Noeekwol sat down in the same seat he had the first time he was brought to the office. When the officer disappeared inside the office, Noeekwol took a moment to look around the busy prison's security room. He noticed a rosy cheeked secretary smiling at him, so he smiled back. Officer Buckley returned.

"Bondz, you can go in now. She's ready for you," he informed him while still standing inside the doorway.

Noeekwol stood up and entered the cozy corner office. He was met by a woman who kind of reminded him of the actress Debra Messing.

She had been busy typing away on the desktop computer's keyboard until he walked in.

"Mr. Bondz." She put on her perfect smile. "Please close the door and have a seat," she said, gesturing toward one of the two genie chairs positioned in front of her desk so an unruly inmate could be easily removed if need be. "How are you doing this afternoon? My name is Captain Lawson. As you already know, I am the security director here at DCI."

"Okay, but why am I here?" he inquired, sitting as instructed.

Lawson took a good look at the inmate seated across from her. Even though he was dressed in the tacky forest green prison uniform, she thought he was handsome.

"Well, as security director, my job is to make sure you, as well as everyone around you, are safe during your stay here at DCI. That also includes my officers," she stated, sounding like a warning. "I've been looking over your record. I see that you're a first timer who received a slap on the wrist for severely beating a Milwaukee police detective with your fists."

"Captain Lawson, that detective shot my unarmed little brother, and I just lost it. I didn't set out to do it."

"I don't care why you did the shit you did, Bondz. I just want you to know that it's not going to be repeated in my prison," she said, interrupting him. "I do not care how big and bad you are when you're outside of these walls fighting in that cage. You're not that person here. If you harm one of my officers or staff

4

members here for any reason, I will press charges and have your little sentence extended by up to ten years. Do you understand?"

"Yes, ma'am, I do, and I want you to know I'm not on that. I'm not a troublemaker," he responded with sincerity.

"Good. Bondz, my best advice to you is to follow my rules and make your time easy. Do the time, and don't let it do you."

"Yes, ma'am."

"Now, if you have any problems with anybody, including staff, I want you to come to me. You can just let any officer know that you would like to speak with me, and I will call you in to see me as soon as I can, or I will come to you," Lawson said, knowing he would not due to the no snitching code that the mass majority of the inmates lived by.

The security director was aware of all of the beatings, extortions, and rapes that took place almost daily. However, she could do very little about most of these incidents, because the victims would not talk, and the ones who did usually did not last much longer in the general population afterward.

"Bondz, per court order, with good behavior you could get released in around eight to ten months, so let's work to make that happen."

"That's my goal as long as no one tries to hurt me. If that happens, I can't promise you that I won't defend myself to the best of my ability. No, I'm telling you now that I won't hesitate to defend myself if that happens," Noeekwol said, thinking about the group of disrespectful white supremacists who tried to intimidate him not long ago.

"Well, for your sake, let's pray nothing like that happens. Good day, Mr. Bondz. You're excused," she immediately dismissed him and went back to work on her computer.

Noeekwol got up and exited the office without saying another word. He found Buckley conversing with the secretary and another female officer. As the champ approached them, he heard the panic alarm start screaming over their radios. Buckley suddenly shot out of the security office and ran at top speed, leaving him standing there.

"Have a seat now!" the female officer yelled before she herded Noeekwol toward the chairs where he had been sitting before his meeting with Lawson.

"Whoa, hold up. You don't gotta push me. I'm going to sit down."

"When you do, sit on your hands!"

"Okay." Once seated the way she ordered him to, he asked her a question. "What's going on? The director said I'm free to return to the cell block?"

"Not right now. Something's happening on one of the cell blocks. As soon as I get the all clear, I'll escort you back. Just please be patient."

About fifteen minutes later, the officer returned and marched Noeekwol back down to his cell block. As he descended the last flight of stairs to the dungeon, Noeekwol noticed all of the extra officers and medical staff that were there. He then saw a large group of inmates all lined up in the dayroom being patted down before being locked in their cells. When he spotted Vet being tended to by two worried looking nurses while he was strapped to a gurney, he picked up his pace.

"Vet!" Noeekwol yelled to get his attention.

"Bondz, no yelling!" his escort said, grabbing him by the arm to slow him down.

"Vet, who did this to you?" he demanded, ignoring the officer's warning while almost dragging her toward his friend.

"Bondz, stop!" Buckley exclaimed, suddenly appearing in front of him. "You can't go over there, and you can't talk to him."

"Buckley, what fuckin' happened to him?" the champ demanded, even more pissed off after seeing Vet's bloody and battered face more clearly.

Both of his eyes were swollen almost shut, and his lips were badly split.

"Man, just go to your cell. I know he's your friend; so when I find out more about what happened, I'll come talk to you. I promise," Buckley muttered in a calm voice while leading him back toward his cell.

"Is this why you left me down there, 'cause you knew what the fuck was going on down here?"

"No, I ran because it's my job. I did not know who it was until I got here; and honestly, it didn't hit me that he was your friend until I heard you calling to him. Look, I got you, man. Just please let me see what I can find out and get back to you?"

Noeekwol agreed just as he noticed that Vet's cellmates were not in the cell when he walked by heading to his.

"Where's his cellies? Was they a part of this?" he inquired while standing at his cell door.

"Neither of them were in the room when the assault took place, from what I know. The room has to be cleaned before they can be allowed back inside. Right now, we have them in a holding cell until it's cleaned," Buckley explained before he yelled for them to close the door.

Directly after the heavy door slammed shut and the officer had gone, Bobby promptly informed Noeekwol of everything he had heard. Bobby told him he had heard the scuffle going on, but he did not know it was coming from Vet's cell. He said when he looked out of the cell to check out what was going on, he saw both of Vet's cellmates briskly walking toward the dayroom for the orientation video.

"So you sayin' you think they did have something to do with it?"

"Champ, I'm willing to put money on it!" Bobby retorted. "I meant what I told y'all earlier, too," he said as he walked over to his bunk and retrieved a five or six inch cruel looking metal shank from beneath his mattress. "I'm strapped and got an L-ball to do whatever. Just tell me the play!" he said sincerely as he gripped his weapon in his hand at his side.

"When is the next time we get to come out for something?" the champ asked him while pacing the small space.

"Man, bro, I really don't know. I'm thinking because of what happened, that shit might have us on movement until dinner or in the morning. We're on lockdown for sure right now," Bobby replied, taking a seat on the edge of his bunk and easing the blade away.

"Fuck it! Whenever these doors break, I'ma go up in there and holla at them lames!"

"Nawl, bro! *We* going up in there to holla at 'em. I don't care how good you is with your hands. I ain't letting you run up in there with two muthafuckas by yo'self!" Bobby corrected him before he lay back on his pillow and watched Noeekwol pace back and forth.

TWO

HEAVEN SPENT THE DAY online learning everything she needed to know so she could be as supportive as she could to her man while he served his prison time. She found out how to add money to his inmate account, so she transferred $500 into it for him. Next, Heaven put together a care package from J.L. Marcus to make Noeekwol's stay a bit more comfortable. The package contained a 13 inch LED TV, a radio, headphones, and a pair of Nike cross trainers, because she knew he liked to work out. Just the thought of Noeekwol's ripped, muscular body dripping in sweat ignited her lust for him. She shook away the thoughts and refocused on getting Noeekwol the rest of what she felt he needed to get started.

She did not send him any type of clothing because she did not want to get anything wrong, so she just sent him stamped envelopes, paper, and pens instead. That way he could send her a list of the rest of the things he needed and wanted.

Once she had finished with her online shopping, Heaven sat propped up on pillows in bed with Noeekwol's laptop sitting on her lap. She tried to come up with the perfect words to put in a letter to him.

She wanted badly to hear his voice, but he had not called like he promised her he would. When she went down to the county jail to visit him, she was informed that he had been transferred to Dodge Correctional Institution. That was five days ago. Now staring at the screen with her half inch French manicured fingers resting on the keyboard, Heaven wondered how she had allowed a man into her heart after all she had been through in her young life. Love was not a part of her plan for her and Noeekwol. He was only supposed to be what she needed to do to survive after his mother had been murdered. All of the sex that she had with him was just her acting out a fantasy. At first. Now the simple thought of Noeekwol's hard, sexy body covering hers made her liver quiver and heart flutter.

She involuntarily wet her lips and allowed her mind to slip back on the last time he touched her intimately. As she reminisced, her hands moved with a mind of their own to her lacy black bra, which then freed her perky breasts. Heaven imagined her hands were his, so each and every time her thumbs brushed across her sensitive nipples, light sparks of pleasure shot through her and awakened the heat deep between her legs. She eased her thumb into her mouth immediately wishing it was her man's thick length that she was sucking and licking on.

Heaven pushed aside the laptop and then slid her free hand down between her knees. She felt the warm tension build as her heart commenced to pound harder and harder, forcing her blood to rush into all of the sweet places. Her fingers slithered inside her slit and found her clit ready to be touched. She worked it, moving her fingers so tenderly back and around that soon her warmth coated her fingers with her wetness. This made her massage it a bit faster, applying more and more pressure with every pass. She let the tips of her nails brush her opening, and she moaned from the pleasure of it. When she pushed them inside of her channel, she clearly pictured Noeekwol's lusty facial expression he always made when he pushed his hardness deep inside her. The memory made her wetter. She thrust her fingers faster while rotating her clit simultaneously faster and faster, until a tidal wave of a climax came down. Her bedding was soaked almost the same as every time Noeekwol had been inside her.

Heaven just lay there stuck in her bliss, until the moment passed and her heart calmed down. Once she regained her composure, she knew just the words to write in the letter to her man. Her man. The admission made her smile like a bride on her wedding day. She retrieved the laptop and began composing the love letter.

* * *

When Nyte was not at Heaven's side assisting her with making sure that the family attorney, Jake, did right with the brothers' nightclub and underground brothels' finances, she spent the rest of her free time sitting in front of a TV at the hospital by her man's side.

Immediately when Beysik's follow-up test was completed, the doctor informed her that it showed positive indicators of improvement in decreasing the massive swelling around his spine. Once Nyte had the okay, she had Jake have Beysik moved out of intensive care and into a private room under Heaven's direction, because she had been left in charge of his care by Noeekwol before he turned himself in.

They all agreed that when Beysik opened his clear hazel gray eyes, that Nyte's face should be the first one he would see. Beysik was the only thing she loved more than sex and money, and she understood that it took money to keep both of them in her life. Nyte used her street smarts and the time she and Heaven were temporarily in charge of their late boss Mercy Bondz's operation to upgrade a few things. Nyte did this so that when Beysik took over, it would be less hassle on everyone.

Nyte deviously came up with a plan to use Detective Allison to get rid of all of the underage girls and boys that were being forced to prostitute inside the brothels by Mercy Bondz's old Albanian partners. They only cared about the money they made and not the ones who made it for them. So she was thinking of a way to break away from having anything at all to do with them, now that Mercy Bondz was dead.

Nyte put together a dream team of whores who wanted to remain in the life of selling sex. She spent money on pampering them to show them that they were truly valued. Nyte knew that the finer the hoe, the richer the tricks would be. This was unlike what the former pimp did, only tending to his workers' basic and cheapest needs, unless one of them brought him a nice bonus of cash or jewelry he could sell. Nyte still planned on doing the same thing. She also pampered them with all of their grooming needs, including everything from wigs to toes, all before putting them back out there to work. She also made sure they all understood that they were now representing Beysik; and if anyone's appearance was not on point for the high end clients that she was assigning to them, they would be put back to work in the cheap brothels. The men and women Nyte had as clients paid very well for discretion and good safe copulation.

* * *

"Nini!"

"Hey, Bey! How are you feeling?" Nyte anxiously inquired as she responded to the nickname that only Beysik used for her.

"Ummmmm, am I in the hospital?" His voice was a scratchy whisper from not being used while in his medically induced comatose state from which he had just awoken. "What happened?" he asked while trying to clear his throat.

"Bey! Bey! Don't you remember any of what happened?"

"Bitch, if I did, I wouldn't be asking you shit. What's up, man? Damn!" he retorted, catching a glimpse of worry in Nyte's face.

"Bey, don't! You don't need to be getting yourself all worked up when you just woke up," she said as she stood up. "I only questioned you because the doctor told me to be on the lookout for signs and stuff with you, like memory loss and any other unusual symptoms, when you woke up," Nyte explained while clutching his cold hand.

"My bad, Nini. I ain't—my head is kinda foggy."

"See, that's from the meds they gave you to put you out."

"Out? Okay now you gotta please tell me why I'm in here," he pleaded, looking around at the heart monitoring apparatus that he was hooked up to and the screen displaying his heart rate and blood pressure.

"Do you remember what happened to Pops and Mama?" she asked.

Within seconds of the question, she witnessed a sadness flood into Beysik's eyes as he recalled the news that the detective had given him at Racine County Jail.

"Yeah, I remember."

"Okay, well you had gone over to their house for some reason afterward. Do you know why you went over there?"

"No." He shook his head. "I can't think, so just tell me."

"Alright! Well you was over there when the Feds busted in the house. One of 'em shot you because he thought you had a gun in your hand, but you didn't. You had the TV remote—that's all. Do you remember that?"

"I got shot?" he mumbled, and then frowned. "Noe? Where is my fuckin brother!" Beysik exclaimed, causing the monitor to beep as he attempted to sit up.

But as soon as he lifted himself up, sharp pains shot through his body. The pain instantly forced him to give up on the task and lie back down wincing in pain.

"No, don't move. You're gonna really hurt yourself," Nyte told him, pressing the red button beside his bed, which gave him a dose of morphine. She then pressed the black one, which called the nurse. "Noeekwol's alright. Just worry about you getting better right now."

18

"What in the fuck does that mean? Nyte, don't lie to me. I remember seeing him jump—!" Beysik then slipped back to sleep before he could finish his drowsy statement.

Nyte adjusted the pillow beneath his head and explained to the nurse everything Beysik had told her he was feeling when he first woke up. She also told her about when he tried to get out of bed and how he was wincing in pain before she pushed the pain med button. Nyte sat back down out of the way so the two nurses could do their jobs and check him over. When Nurse Brenda informed Nyte that all looked well with him, it settled her nerves again.

Nyte turned the television back on. She did not have any pressing work to do at the club, and if she had, it would have to wait because she could not leave Beysik's side now that he was awake from the medical induced coma. Before she sat back into the recliner and allowed herself to get caught up on the show *Empire*, she sent Heaven a text to let her know that Beysik had woken up but then fallen back asleep.

THREE

IT WAS MIDAFTERNOON when the lockdown on the dungeon was lifted due to Vet's assault a week ago. Since a man was found beaten, bloodied, and unconscious on the floor of his cell with no witnesses, Captain Lawson ordered it to be locked down. She did it so anyone that felt some way about the incident and wanted to retaliate could use the time to calm down. She also needed to give her officers time to do their investigation.

Vet was so severely beaten that he had to be taken to an off grounds hospital for surgery. One of his broken ribs had punctured his lung, which made the gang beating an outside assault and battery case for the Disciple that Vet had stabbed in the leg. Since the Disciple was the one in an unassigned area, Vet was not charged with the stabbing. The young thug barely escaped being transferred to the super max prison located in Boscobel, Wisconsin.

Noeekwol was unaware of anything other than the fact that Vet was rushed to the hospital. So he and Bobby used the lockdown time to plan their next move. Bobby's suggestion for retaliation was to wait until movement was restored, so they could go to the chow hall and find out exactly who was involved. He needed to know who they were up against. But the champ did not care who had Vet's former cellmates' backs in the prison. Noeekwol agreed with Bobby's suggestion, but he had no intention to wait until after chow time. He also did not have much faith in Bobby to have his back for real.

The champ could not understand how Bobby did not know that three Disciples were in the cell jumping Vet, when he knew from their lunch conversation that Vet's cellmates had animosity with him from the streets.

"Line up for chow!" the unit officer bellowed from behind his desk in the corner of the cell block.

Noeekwol was up and dressed and already pacing the cell when he heard the announcement. It was go time for him. He threw on his boots, tied them up tight, and was eager to pounce. When the cell door slid open, he rushed out and straight into the cell of the two unsuspecting men. Noeekwol caught them both sitting on their bunks pulling on their boots.

"Oh shit!" they exclaimed in unison at the sight of the furious MMA light heavyweight champ who now had his rage focused on them.

Noeekwol sprang into action before their surprise faded. He slammed a stiff right jab into the mouth of the first one that jumped to his feet. The champ then followed it up with a ferocious three piece combination. The combination ended up with a light, quick side kick to the solar plexus of the man's cellie who tried to rush up from behind. Noeekwol's kick sent him crashing into the corner, right where the steel bunk bed frame and the cold brick wall met. That gave the Disciple time to roll away and get to his feet. He fought back the best he could. He threw savage haymakers at the champ's head, which he easily blocked with his forearms while smiling fiendishly. Noeekwol hit the untrained fool with an uppercut that broke the man's jaw on contact, followed by a hard right cross that knocked him on his ass.

"Stop! Stop! Get back in your cell now!" one of the two officers assigned to the cell block shouted at Bobby, who was awestruck watching Noeekwol in action from the doorway.

"Stop it now! Let him go!" the second officer yelled at Noeekwol, who he had only seen holding up the battered man by the collar of his bloody, torn shirt.

"Whoa, whoa now!" he yelled as he fell off the bunk. "I'm just trying to help him," Noeekwol lied while instantly releasing the dazed man and putting his hands up in surrender.

The officer marched into the cell and aggressively seized the champ by his arm and shirt.

"Let's go! Move!" he ordered.

Noeekwol took a quick calming breath and then allowed the foolish prison guard to pull him from standing over his victim and out of the cell. As soon as the officer had him in the dayroom, Noeekwol was surrounded, handcuffed, and then pat searched for weapons.

"What happened in here?" the shift captain, who had been called to the disturbance on the reception unit, asked.

"They fell!" Noeekwol answered unconvincingly.

The captain rolled his eyes and repeated the question to the two battered men in the cell. Noeekwol stood up tall while straining to hear how they answered.

"We were horseplaying and fell off the bunk," the man said, still holding his face as he recovered from the powerful kick. "He was just trying to help us up!"

"What in the hell do you take me for? Do I fucking look stupid to you?" the captain bellowed, snatching him up by his arm. "Okay, so that's how y'all want to play this?" He turned to his officers and said, "Have them cleaned by HSU and then toss 'em in seg on TLU until I find out what's really going on down there," he ordered before storming past the champ with a grin on his face.

The officers placed the two bangers in handcuffs and then moved them all to the Health Services unit so the nurse could bandage them up. The one with the broken jaw went out to the hospital, and the other followed Noeekwol straight to the segregation unit, where they were placed on temporary lockdown for investigation just like the captain had ordered.

* * *

Nyte was reenergized by the knowledge that her man would soon be going home from the hospital. To Nyte, Beysik deserved the best of everything, because he was the only one who seemed to care about her. That was the only reason she was going on the date with a new drug connect for Rich. She knew it would help Beysik as well, if all went well, but she could not understand why Rich did not negotiate using one of the other girls. She wondered if she was silly for thinking that Rich was trying to put bad blood between her and Beysik. Her cold streetsmart intuition was warning her to leave this deal alone, but she could not trust it at the moment because of her ill feelings for Rich in the first place.

Nyte stopped at the stoplight and checked the address she had stored in her phone before she went on to the meeting place. She pulled up to the cheap motel on South 108 and National Avenue and parked. Nyte texted the number and told them she was there. Then she just sat in the car because they had not given her a room number with the address. About fifteen minutes passed, and Nyte was trying her best not to pull off. She kept reminding herself that she was doing this for Beysik. Nyte could not wait until he was home so she could wake up in his strong arms the way she used to. A heavyset, biracial, light skinned man dressed in a nice business suit walked out of one of the rooms and approached her car.

"Are you Rich's girl?" he asked when she lowered the window.

"Are you his boy?" she retorted, not liking being called Rich's girl, as if Rich was running things.

She started to call off the date; but instead, she just got out of the car and followed him inside while telling herself that this was her last time. Nyte also planned on telling Beysik about this, as well as all the other bullshit Rich had been pulling since Noeekwol told him to help them until he woke up and got out of the hospital.

"I hope he told you that I expect to be tipped up front," she informed the man as soon as she stepped foot in the room.

FOUR

IN SEG, NOEEKWOL QUICKLY found out what it really meant to be one with himself. After spending the first two and a half days just sleeping and eating. He decided to make better use of the dead time. On the secure housing unit, time really had no meaning, because there was no movement except to the shower stalls every other day. Other than that, all meals were brought to his cell and shoved through a tray door in the middle of the steel cell door three times a day. But he was lucky to get a cell right across from the large wall clock. He only used it to time his workout sessions, which were made up of calisthenics and martial arts exercises.

"Well, I'm the dough boy, and the one they're talking about. All these gossiping ass niggas got my name in their mouth. I know the bad bitches, but know niggas who are bitches, too. They should bleed once a month 'cause that's what these bitches do. You a bitch and yo' bitch should expose you."

Noeekwol rapped Yo Gotti songs in between his pushup sets. He had just dropped down and started pushing out his tenth set of fifty reps, when in the midst of the set he heard the trapdoor being opened. It was not meal time, because lunch had just been served a little over two hours ago, and the book cart did not come around until after dinner, so he paused to see what was going on. Noeekwol was hoping they were coming to tell him that his TLU time was now up, so he could find out what was going on with his friend, Vet.

"Bondz, you got mail!" the officer announced as he tossed an envelope through the trapdoor and then slammed it shut extra hard.

The envelope landed facedown, not far from where Noeekwol was holding his pushup position. So the champ was still left to wonder who it was from until he finished his set. He banged out the last thirty reps and then snatched up the envelope. He smiled when he saw that it was from Heaven.

He anxiously peeled open the tape used to reseal the envelope after it was opened and inspected for contraband by the mailroom staff. The sweet aroma of Heaven's perfume filled the air as soon as he removed the letter. Noeekwol took a deep sniff of the pages as he sat on the floor slumped against the wall and read.

Dear Noe,

The weirdest thing happened to me this morning. I woke up with tears in my eyes and one rolling down in a stream on my cheek. I know I must've been dreaming of you again. I do my best to hide my tears when Nyte or your little sisters and brothers talk about you, but the pain I feel is still the same. Although I put on a smile and seem carefree, there's no one who misses you more than me. I can't wait 'til I can roll over in this bed and kiss you good morning instead of lying here typing this letter to send in the mail to you. Sometimes I just wish you were here so I could show you how much I need you and how hard every day has been without you. I want to tell you about my day, I want to laugh with you about yours. But mostly, I want all of the days to start and end the same—with you here.

I am so emotionally crazed by missing you. I look at all of your fights and training videos when I'm missing you so much, and I just smile like an idiot. I listen to all the songs that remind me of us, and then I fight back tears and miss you more. I want to fall asleep with you whispering "I love you" in my ear. I hate days like this when I can feel every mile between us. Noe, I didn't want to fall in love ever, at all. But at some point, you smiled, and holy shit, I blew it! LOL!

Hey, question? Do you believe that someone can become so damaged that when that one tries to give you what you deserve in life, you have no fucking idea how to respond? I think that's me. SMH! Hey, isn't it strange how there's so many people out here who are secretly in love with someone, and there are so many people that have no idea that they are loved. I said that to say that I wish I had spoken up way sooner and not been so scared of everything. I doubted myself because I worked for Mama and Pops. I used to ask myself: Why would this man want me? Tell me, do you think there's more magic in the words "I miss you" than "I love you." Hey, there's so much I want to know about you and I want you to know about me. So let's play the question game in our next letters, and we have to be honest and open, and nothing is off of the table to ask.

Okay, Noe, I gotta end this rant so I can get up out of this bed and get ready. Nyte will be here soon, so we can go open up the club, because her ass is texting me right now. Noe, I need to say this. Your boy, Rich, is a trip. Well, write back.

I sent you money and a care package to get you started in there. I didn't know what all to get, so send me a list of anything I forgot, and I'll send it to you ASAP. Be good in there so you can come back home to me when you're supposed to, and send me a visiting form so I can come see you. Bye for now.

Yours always,

Heaven

All Noeekwol could do when he finished reading the letter was sit there with his head on his forearms, grinning and thinking of Heaven lying naked across the bed with the laptop typing the letter to him. The fantasy of her sexy body was arousing him. His erection pressed against its prison of the bright orange seg pants. Noeekwol thought of whipping it out and stroking until it released; but instead, he tossed the letter onto the bed and got back down on the floor to finish out his pushups while thinking of his reply.

FIVE

THE POLICE CHIEF SUMMONED Detective Allison to his office and demanded an update on her current homicide case. Needless to say, the beating Noeekwol had put on Detective Sadd, which forced him into early retirement, sent the Bondz homicides to the bottom of his to do list. The true blue captain did not care to reward anyone in any way for hurting one of his officers. So he interrupted when Tabitha brought the thumbprint that was found on one of the spent shell casings that was collected from the crime scene.

He was about to dismiss her, when the desk sergeant entered the office and informed them of a couple of callers claiming to be eyewitnesses to the Michigan Street massacre. They had just called in about the reward money that was being offered for information that could help catch the killer.

"Medley, do you believe they're legit?" the chief asked, quickly forgiving his sergeant for just barging into his office.

"I do, sir. Both have said things that have not been released to the public."

"Alright then," the chief said while stirring his coffee. "Allison, are you up to going out to interview these two?"

"Sure, all he has to do is forward me their names and addresses," Tabitha responded, standing up from the chair across from the chief.

"There's no need, Detective. I've asked them to come into the station to give sworn statements. It's my way of weeding out the ones who really have info for us over the ones who are just trying to scam us out of the reward money," Medley arrogantly explained, hoping to impress his superior.

"Sergeant, how long have you been using that method of yours?" Tabitha inquired while frowning in amazement.

"I've been using it for maybe six months, give or take a week."

"So for six months you've been turning away callers who may have useful info that could solve the growing pile of homicide cases that are sitting on my desk right now, by telling them to come into the station without getting their personal contact information? Sergeant! As a detective who is out in the field every day, I can tell you that your method is flawed. People out there don't trust police, and the ones who do, don't want to be caught talking to us out of fear for their lives or the lives of their family members."

"Allison's right, Sergeant! I cannot have that kind of negligence manning the phones. Get your things and report down to the garage for duty."

"Hold up! Are you serious, Capt.?" the stunned former desk sergeant asked, approaching the captain's desk.

"I don't joke on the clock, because this isn't the place for it. I also do not joke about my job protecting this city. Now, report to the garage and let Franklin know she's taking over for you. Dismissed!"

"But, Capt.!"

"I said dismissed, Medley. It is best that you leave my office before you find yourself on two weeks' suspension without pay for your negligence on the job and for disobeying orders. So it's the garage or home. Your choice?" the chief exclaimed, now standing with his face brushed with anger awaiting the officer's answer.

"I'll go to the garage," he conceded shamefully before marching out of the office.

Tabitha did not want to be a part of the demotion of a fellow officer. Her only intent in expressing her mind was to make Medley see the colossal error in the way he was doing his job.

"Sir, I don't want to overstep and put my foot in my mouth for a second time. So I'm going to talk about myself," Tabitha spoke up after the angry sergeant had gone. "Capt. I—!" she paused briefly, trying to find the right words.

"What about you, Detective?" he pressed as he dropped down in his seat and picked up his #1 Dad coffee mug to have a sip.

"I don't believe I handled that right with the sergeant."

"Why is that? You should express your concerns, especially when it's about the job. Who knows how much time Medley's actions have cost us."

"That's true, but I should've addressed him one on one first, and then given him time or the chance to correct himself instead of saying something in front of you," Tabitha said, shifting her weight. "Right now I'm without a partner. On top of that, I'm still fairly new around here. No one is going to want to work with me once he's done trashing me for how I just threw him under the bus with you."

"I see your concern. Tell me, Allison, how do you think we can fix this?"

"I'm sure Medley will no longer be using his old methods of answering the phones, so I don't believe he should lose his position at the desk permanently. There has to be another way to penalize him that doesn't include him losing pay or the desk."

"You know what, Allison, you're right. I'll handle this with him. You just go get ready to interview the witnesses when they arrive."

"Sir, can I ask what you are going to do with him?"

"I'm going to send him to the 911 training class for the weekend. Hopefully when he returns, he will know how to take calls," the chief told her before he tapped his computer to life, giving it his attention while dismissing her.

The detective understood that meant he had nothing more to say, so she withdrew herself from the office. When she headed for her desk, she caught a few disapproving stares from a few of her coworkers. Tabitha knew those were the ones who had obviously been told the story about how she had thrown the sergeant under the bus a little while ago with the chief.

Before she made it to her work station, Tabitha spotted Medley across the squad room standing at the water cooler venting about his demotion to a few more of his buddies. She took a few deep breaths and then counted down from five before exhaling the last one. She then briskly marched over to apologize to him. She also planned to give him the heads up about the new plan for him instead of him being demoted.

As soon as Tabitha was a few feet in front of the sergeant, his replacement, Officer Franklin, intercepted and informed her that the witnesses had arrived for her. Franklin then told Medley that the chief wanted to see him in his office ASAP.

"Excuse me, Medley. I want you to know that I didn't m—!"

"Fuck you, Detective!" he spat. "What did you do now? Talk him into taking my shield?" he exclaimed before he then shoulder checked her as he stomped past her.

He bumped her so hard he almost knocked her over.

"Okay, I guess I deserved that," Tabitha said aloud, shaking her head before turning back to address Officer Franklin. "Franklin, if Rooms 3 and 4 are available, could you have one placed in each? And since I'm without a partner, I'm going to need you in there with me. I'll be at my desk when you have them ready," she said, all business, before heading back to her desk.

Once there, she quickly put together an interview file while taking a moment for herself.

SIX

TABITHA NAVIGATED HER CRUISER through the busy rush of traffic and headed toward the hospital. She played the recording of the witness interviews that she had conducted just forty three minutes earlier. She listened intently while the smudgy looking Caucasian female gave her account of her time spent inside the dope house. The witness stated that she had seen an unknown black man come out of what she believed to be the basement's entrance, because the layout of the kitchen was very similar to that of her own home. She said she did not know at the time that the man had killed T. Rod, who was sitting at the table like always. The witness said she thought the man had punched T. Rod and then quickly made his way over to the stairs that led to the upper level. The woman stated that she only caught a glimpse of the side of his face as he crossed the poorly lit room. He then disappeared onto the second floor. She said it was not long after that, that she heard the exchange of gunfire, and then the same man came flying through the banister.

She said he landed on the sofa below, bounced back up onto his feet, and began to shoot as he ran from the house.

Tabitha turned onto the hospital grounds just as her first witness's interview concluded. She found a parking spot marked Officials Only, and pulled into the reserved parking slot just as the interview of her second witness's recording began.

Her second witness also claimed to have been inside the building where the massacre had taken place. He was a Mexican American male that the detective could very clearly tell was an addict. He also looked just as mangy and smudgy as his girlfriend. He described the murder scene from a slightly different point of view, which made Tabitha believe that they were telling her the truth. But Sergeant Medley had one thing right: the couple was trying to pull one over on the system by calling in separately so they could collect a bigger cut of the reward money. But from the way the sergeant had treated her at the water cooler, Tabitha was not going to tell him that.

Witness number two stated that he was only trying to get out of harm's way when the gun battle started. He said and repeated that he did not, in any way, hurt anyone that night. He then went on to state that a young looking black man known as Booky was working the door of the spot. Out of nowhere, Booky came rushing toward him with his gun drawn. The witness stated that he dove out of his path to avoid being shot when Booky fired a mess of shots at someone by the couch at the back of the room. The witness said that he was still lying on the floor when the doorman's body jerked and dropped awkwardly to the floor from the two or three times he was shot. Then an unknown man leaped over him and the body as he ran out the door. Once the man was outside, the witness said he heard more gunfire being exchanged out there.

Both eyewitnesses were able to pick MJ out of Tabitha's photo lineup, but only the second witness was able to pick out Fame, who was the detective's suspect who she was now going into the hospital to talk to. Even though the second witness had recognized Fame, he said that he was not 100 percent sure and could not say with real certainty that he was her man. So now Tabitha hoped she could scare Fame a bit and make him confess to his deeds.

* * *

Beysik was alone pretty much for the first time since he had woken up, and he was completely relaxed sitting propped up in bed watching reruns of the TV show *Blackish*. He was beginning to drift in and out of sleep from the cocktail of medications that he was given fifteen minutes earlier. Beysik was about to give in to the meds when Heaven showed up to check in on him.

"Hey, Bey, how are you feeling today?" she asked while walking over to his bed side.

"Hey, what up?" he responded weakly, eyeing the nurse that had followed Heaven into the room. "Where's Nyte? Is she comin'?"

"She's at my crib knocked the fuck out, all snoring like a baby. Your auntie called me and asked me to help her put together a birthday party for Mimi, so I just let Nyte sleep in. Her ass is gonna need it, because she got another busy night at the club and stuff for us. And you know that her ass ain't going to wanna miss out on nothin'!" Heaven explained.

A knock on the door drew everyone's attention to the entrance where the detective happily invited herself into the room.

42

"Hi, Detective," the nurse greeted. "Is everything alright with Mr. W, or do you need me for something else?" she asked while still examining Beysik's dressings.

"Oh no, everything's fine with him, Brenda. I'm actually here for Mr. Bondz. I hope this isn't too bad of a time," Tabitha responded.

"Not if you're not here to tell us that you caught them. I have not heard anything else about nothing since your partner shot him, and y'all put Noeekwol in prison behind it," Heaven vented, walking over to meet Tabitha at the door to stop her advancing any further into the room.

"I assure you that I'm working hard to find the ones behind those murders. I know that what my old partner did to your family has cost me your trust. But believe me, I was against Sadd raiding your home, and, frankly, he got what he deserved for what he did," Tabitha explained in a hushed voice. "I'm just trying to do my job and close these cases the right way."

"So you do have something for us?" Heaven inquired in the same hushed tone.

"No, not yet! I was here visiting another person of interest in an unrelated case, when I remembered Bondz was here."

"So what, you're just visiting him then?"

"Actually, I have some suspect photos that I would like him to take a look at," the detective replied.

"For what? Beysik wasn't there when it happened, I was," Heaven reminded her, still very suspicious of the sudden visit.

"Well, I know that he was close to his father. I think he may be able to tell me of anyone who would want to see his mother and father dead. It would help if you took a look at them as well."

Nothing about the detective being there seemed right to Heaven.

It was a real coincidence that she just happened to be in the hospital on the first day Nyte was not by Beysik's side. Heaven did not trust Tabitha. She still believed that the Feds were trying to build a case against them, even though Mercy Bondz was dead.

"I was told by your lawyer not to talk to y'all without him, and I'm sure he means that for Beysik, too."

"It's just a few photos that I want you two to take a look at—nothing else, and it wouldn't take long," Tabitha pressed.

Beysik was eyeing the two women as the nurse checked him over, no doubt being nosy herself. Beysik recognized the sexy detective right away from when she delivered the news of his parents' murder to him in the Racine jail. Even though he could not hear what the detective was talking to Heaven about, he could make out from Heaven's body language that it was not a conversation he wanted to be a part of, at least not until he was back on his feet. So he told the nurse in his best groggy whisper that he was too sleepy to talk to anyone.

"Excuse me? I know you two just got here, but the medication is taking effect on him now, and he needs to rest without stress so it can do its job," the nurse said, approaching the women to usher them out of the room.

"Brenda, I only have a couple of quick questions for him. I only need a moment."

"I'm sorry, Detective, but he's fresh out of intensive care, and too much stress could put him back, so I'm going to have to decline your request for now."

"How about you call our lawyer and set something up with him to meet here later on tomorrow sometime? But if you're not trying to trick me and all you really want is for me to see if I recognize some people in some photos, I'll do that for you now on the way out to the parking lot," Heaven said as she led Tabitha away from Beysik's room.

Heaven only agreed to look at the photos so she could do some investigating of her own. If she did see someone she knew in one of them, then she would have something to report to Noeekwol about it—or better yet, when she went to visit him.

"Alright, let's do it!" Tabitha agreed after removing a tan file folder from her soft black leather briefcase while they waited for the elevator to arrive.

SEVEN

HEY GORGEOUS,

I got your letter the other day, but I couldn't write back until now. Your letter made me remember when my dad was locked up when I was a kid. I remember seeing my mama writing in a red notebook all the time and sitting on her bed reading his letters, just smiling and even crying sometimes. I never thought I would be doing this prison shit myself. But here I am. SMH! I'm glad I have someone like my mama to hold me down the way she did for my dad. Thank you!

Anyway, I'm just now writing back because I'm in the box, and I didn't know that I was allowed to have pen, paper, and two free stamped envelopes a month in here until today. Oh, just in case you don't know what the box is—it's segregation. But don't get all worried and shit. I'm fine. They're investigating some bullshit that went down on the cell block, that's all. I'll tell you about it one day, just not now.

So you really love me, huh? They say that doing time will show you who's with you and who's not. It shows you what kinda woman you got out there, and if she's worth making wherever she is home or not. This is still early for us, but from the way you're handling things now, I feel it's gonna be all good with us.

Oh yeah, Heaven, I don't get property in the box, so I don't know if the stuff you sent made it here or not yet. But I'll let you know as soon as it do.

I can't lie, but I'm missing you like crazy, too, especially right now writing this letter. You know what? I think that the fact that my mama had you around her all the time is what makes you the perfect woman for me. My mama—RIP—is the perfect woman in my world. So I hope you learned something from her?

Heaven, I think playing your question game would be good for us, too. It's ladies first, so you start it off. I promise to answer your inquiries the best I can and with honesty. Okay, now since I got to send visiting forms, I'ma cut this short so I'll have room for them. Please tell Auntie and the kids I said hi and I miss them much. You stay sweet, and know that my dreams are filled with you.

Always,
Noeekwol Bondz

After writing the letter and sealing the envelope with a kiss, he slid it under the cell door to be picked up when the guard did his rounds through the cell block. Now with nothing else to do, Noeekwol killed time by going through a few martial arts movements to keep his skills fluid. He imagined that the pinkish seg socks he wrapped around his fists were the pair of old boxing gloves his father gave him when he was about four years old. This memory put Noeekwol in an emotional zone.

He started throwing super quick fist, elbow, and knee combinations while repeating, "If you don't see red, then you ain't doing it right."

This was something Mercy Bondz would say to him whenever he stopped by the gym to watch him train.

The sudden sound of the guard opening the trap snapped him out of his zone.

"Bondz! Take a break. Do you want a shower? It sure looks like you need one," the officer yelled through the door.

"Yeah!" he retorted. While toweling off his sweat with his T-shirt before pulling it back on, he stepped over to the window of the cell door and asked, "Hey, did you pick up my letter?"

"I picked it up like an hour ago," he answered, and then moved on.

"Damn! Okay, thanks!"

The champ was surprised that he had let the time get away from him like that while shadowboxing.

"You're up, Bondz. You know the drill. Step to the door and place your hands through the trap," a new officer ordered.

He did as he was told and was cuffed before they opened the cell door to escort him to the shower stall. Once there, he was locked inside before they removed the cuffs and turned the water on for him. Surprisingly, the soft spray of hot, hard water felt wonderful after his intense workout. Noeekwol stood under the water with tears of heartbreak and grief streaming down his cheeks as he said goodbye to his parents once again.

"Bondz, you gotta cut it short. The security director wants to see you."

"Alright, I'm ready now!" he informed the officer, then held his face up to the shower head to clear his tears before the water was shut off.

After drying off and dressing in fresh seg clothes, he allowed the two officers to cuff him again and shackle him.

They escorted him right past his cell and down the stairs to the main floor of the cell block. Noeekwol thought he would be marched out through the main corridor down to the security office like before; but to his disappointment, he never left the SHU. He was taken to a conference room where Captain Lawson sat behind a long folding table reading his incident report.

"Have a seat, Bondz. How is your stay in seg?" she patronized him.

"It's okay, I guess. It's really no different than where I was before," he responded sincerely as he dropped into the seat across the table in front of her.

"That's surprisingly not the answer I expected to hear. Hmmm! Now according to the report, you were involved in the assault of two inmates inside of their cell on your way to the chow hall. Is that correct?"

"No, it's not!"

"Okay, tell me what is?" she asked him while picking up a pen to take notes.

"I didn't assault anyone. Them two were like that when I found them."

"So what happened to them, Mr. Bondz?"

"I don't know, I guess they fell. That's what I heard one of 'em tell the officer anyway. Look, I was just trying to go to chow and saw they needed some help," he explained with a slight grin.

"That's what the two of them told me as well," she chuckled. "Bondz, I won't allow inmates to run around assaulting other inmates. You don't get to run my house. I do. I've been doing this job for far too long to believe that story you guys are telling. I know this was retaliation for what happened to the young man earlier last month. I'm telling you now, Bondz, that this stops here! Do you understand me, sir?" she said, staring him in his eyes.

"Captain, if you need me to say yes, I will; but whatever happened last month has nothing to do with me. If you remember, I was in your office meeting with you when that all went down. It was all over by the time I got back there. So it had nothing to do with me. Lawson, all I know is if it's gonna be all this, I bet you I won't help nobody else."

"Okay, since you're sticking to your statement, I'm going to release the hold on you and have you placed on unit 20 until a bed opens at 3:00. Do you have an issue with this?"

"No, I just thought those blocks were for GP inmates that have been staffed here. I haven't been to staffing yet, so how am I going?"

"I waved your staffing to keep you here at DCI, since you don't have much time to serve. Trust me when I say that you would rather be here than at any other max prison. The only thing is if you stay here, I don't want no more BS out of you. Is that clear?"

"Very."

"Bondz, like I said before, you will be charged if you are involved in something like this again and we can prove that they were seriously hurt by them hands of yours. So please keep them to yourself."

EIGHT

HEAVEN STOOD IN FRONT of the black and purplish blue granite top vanity counter mirror in her bathroom fighting boredom. She started applying the Aveeno Max Glow peel off mask to her already radiant face. Nyte had given her the tube after raving about how the soy, kiwi, and alpha hydroxy acids in it for brightening and exfoliating made her skin feel. So this morning while she waited for Nyte to come over, Heaven decided to do some experimenting with the mask, so she could give Nyte and the others a review of her own experience.

When Heaven was done applying the peel off, she stared blankly at the green glop all over her face and then burst out laughing at her reflection.

"I wonder what Noe would say if he walked in and saw me looking like this?" she asked her reflection in the large free framed mirror. That thought made her go check the mailbox for a reply letter from her man. The box was empty. Heaven checked the time on her Fitbit and saw that it was still early. So with Noeekwol on her mind again, and with nothing else to do but wait, she went into the kitchen and fixed herself a bowl of granola and almond milk. She then got the laptop and plunged into drafting her next letter to Noeekwol.

Good Morning, my King!

I hope you are doing good. It's killing me not hearing from you and, even more, not having you here in my arms. If this shit keeps up, I'ma be a haggard bitch when you come home. LOL!

I don't want to sound like a broken record, buuut I miss you so much! I haven't gotten your letter yet, so I'm not going to say too much. In fact, I am just going to start our game with my list of questions.

1. *What are the two biggest lessons you've learned from your previous relationships?*
2. *What did you learn a little too late?*
3. *What things are you too hard on yourself for?*
4. *What do most people overestimate or underestimate about you?*
5. *What do you love about me?*
6. *What is something you probably should do but never will?*

7. *What was the best mistake you've made?*
   What mistake turned out really good?
8. *What makes you nervous?*
9. *What was the last thing that made you cry?*
10. *Do you trust anyone with your life?*
11. *Do you really believe in love?*
12. *What is something you're embarrassed that*
   you're good at?
13. *Who is the last person you kissed?*
14. *What should I know about you that I would*
   never think to ask?
15. *Have you ever had a secret admirer?*
16. *Have you ever given up on someone but*
   then gone back to them for another round?
17. *Would you kiss the last person that you*
   kissed again?
18. *What is your favorite part of a woman's*
   body?
19. *Name five people whose hearts you've*
   broken and why?
20. *What is your kindest memory of your mom*
   and dad?
21. *Do you really believe I love you the way I*
   say I do?

Well that's it for now. I went easy on you. The deal is that you have to answer them all honestly. I can't wait to see what questions you have for me. Noe, I hope you sent me the visiting form so I can come get me a bunch of your hugs and kisses. Bye bye for now!

Yours,

Heaven

Heaven completed her list of questions and finished her light breakfast. She was happy with her review of the inquiries, because she did not want to make them too serious. But at the same time, she wanted to learn all she could about him due to the strong emotional attachment she felt for him and the whole Bondz family.

A short time had passed from Heaven finishing the letter, and Nyte barged into the house breaking Heaven's train of thought.

"Don't come in here unless you brought me something to smoke," Heaven greeted her while doing a mental analysis of Nyte's outfit.

She was wearing a tiny icy white Finders Keepers dress with slightly puffy sleeves that stopped at the elbow with sparkling gold triangle shaped buttons running down the dress's center. She saw that Nyte had set it off with flashy gold and ruby Lagos chain link jewelry and slim gold Aldo stiletto sandals. The outfit made her look as if she had stepped off a catwalk.

"I got you covered, sis," Nyte said as she dropped her soft, white leather gold and ruby Aldo bag onto the table. "I see you finally tried that kiwi mask. What do you think about it?" she inquired while sitting down across from her and fishing out a sack of weed and wraps from her purse.

"Hmmm, it's tight."

"That's because it's time to peel it off," Nyte replied as she reached over the table and touched Heaven's face. "How long have you had it on?"

"I don't know. A while."

"Ooooh, girl, let me pull it off. I wanna see if I can take it off your face in one piece!"

"I don't care! Go for it!" Heaven agreed, closing down the laptop to keep Nyte out of her and Noeekwol's personal business. "How long have you been back, and how come you ain't called me and let me know something?"

"I didn't call you because Wilson don't like me to use my phone too much when we're together. His ole supersecution complex having ass is afraid of being set up or blackmailed. He's crazy, because he took me out with him last night to see the *Hamilton* play in Chicago. There was a bunch of people there who knew him and his wife that seen us together, but he pays good and I don't gotta fuck him, so fuck it," she explained while sparking up the blunt.

"Yeah, the right amount of cash can make a nightmare a dream. So how was the play? Was it the one with Lin-Manuel Miranda in it, or the knockoff team?"

"Yeah, he was there. I made Wilson pay for me to take pictures with them all since I couldn't take selfies with my own phone. I forgot 'em in the car, damn!" Nyte cursed after checking her bag for the photos. "The play was good though. He had us seated in like the fourth row from the stage. I honestly did not think I would like it all that much, but I did. It's really good for real though. I see why everyone's been talking about on TV," Nyte said, pausing to take another pull off the blunt before passing it over to Heaven.

"Yeah, it's good for all of the folks who didn't pay attention in history class," Heaven retorted as she accepted the weed. She took a strong drag off of it and then continued. "That hip hop play makes *Hamilton* out to be a good guy, when the truth is that he was a dirty slave owning muthafucka, too. Hell, if I remember right, the Hamilton's family business sold slaves and killed hundreds of Natives just like the rest of them white son of a bitches were doing back then."

"Haaaater!" Nyte sang with a giggle.

"I'm not hate'n! It's the truth. You can look it up."

"Girl, I'm just joking with you. All that history shit ain't my thang. I just liked the way the rap flowed and the way the show was put together. I bet you would enjoy it for what it is, if you seen it live yourself."

"I don't know, maybe. It's hard to unknow stuff when you do. Oh yeah, before I forget. That detective bitch came up to the hospital trying to get into the room to talk to Bey, but I stopped her ass right at the door. Then the nurse told us both we were doing too much, so we had to leave so he could get his rest."

"Then what did she do?" Nyte questioned, now on the edge of her seat.

"She asked me to look at some photos of some dudes, and then asked me if I'd ever seen Pops, Mama, or Beysik around any of 'em."

"What did you tell her, Heavens?"

"Nothing, Nyte! I know better than to say something," Heaven said as she rolled her eyes. "I told the bitch to call Jake and set something up with him before she tried to talk to Bey again, or I'll have Jake sue her ass for fuckin' with us. I did look at the pictures just to see if I knew anybody in 'em," she confessed. "I didn't really. I mean one of 'em looked like I may have seen him with Pops before, but I ain't too sure. And, no, I didn't tell her that either."

"Okay! That bitch is getting on my last one! I gotta give her ass some shit to make her leave us the fuck alone before she tries and puts a case on Bey."

"What do you have in mind for her?"

"I don't know yet, but I got something for her ass. Right now, let's just go get that off of your face so I can tell you I told you so. I need to think on the shit before I go and get up with the detective," Nyte said, pulling Heaven out of her chair and towing her into the bathroom so she could remove the Aveeno mask from her face.

NINE

AFTER RECEIVING A FEW credible threats from the Williams family's legal advisor, Tabitha's commanding officer ordered her to allow Asad into the hospital room to visit his brother. From this bold first encounter with her suspect's older brother, Tabitha felt he was going to be a problem for her while trying to get a confession out of Fame so she could close the Michigan Street case.

"You gotten minutes, and the door stays open."

"No, I got fifteen minutes to visit in private, or do I have to call your captain and have him confirm it for you?" Asad threatened.

"You can have the time, but the door stays open. You're lucky I am even allowing you to go into the room alone with him. So if that's not private enough for you, you can have your lawyer call my captain and we can try this all again tomorrow?" she challenged.

"Come on, really now? Tomorrow, Detective?"

"Or later, depending on my workload or if I feel like using a few of my sick days," Tabitha said, holding the frown on her face but wanting to laugh at his. "So take it, or leave it?"

"I'm good. Just don't stand in the doorway," Asad conceded as he walked past her.

As soon as he entered the cool sterile room and saw Fame lying in the bed, memories of the violent beating that he had received at All Stars Night club flashed in his mind. The memory momentarily caused Asad to involuntarily hesitate as the vision came to his mind of a man exploding out of the crowd charging right at him with his head down like a bull. Asad remembered pushing his girlfriend, China, out of the way as he sidestepped and caught the man with a hard knee to the face. The knee sent his assailant crashing to the floor, bloodied and dazed. The next vision was of him being snaked from behind by another man, and then a bunch of hard fists that quickly turned into feet to his head and body before he blacked out.

"Asad? Asad?" Fame yelled, snapping Asad out of the hellish visions. "You good, bro?"

"Yeah, yeah, yeah! I'm good!" he stuttered. "I just had a flashback of when I was fighting for my life in one of these places," he explained while shaking off the lingering thought and putting on a smile.

"I was wondering when you was gonna show up. Did my mama tell you not to come up here like I said?"

"Yeah, she did, but I wouldn't be a good brother if I didn't. Man, I had to go through a lot of shit for this visit, so let's not waste it on what you didn't want. I got my lawyer working on trying to get you outta this jam. Man, bro, the shit they're trying to charge you with don't make any sense to me. Why was you in a stolen car, and how come you didn't tell me about your beef with MJ? I could've handled it for you," Asad inquired in a low voice while standing at Fame's bedside to be sure the detective did not overhear their conversation.

She was out in the hall, where he knew she was listening.

Fame laughed, winched in pain, took a few breaths, and then chuckled some more.

"You really don't know about me, do you?"

"I really don't know what? And stop laughing before you really hurt yourself, ole crazy ass boy!"

"I didn't have beef with them ho ass niggas, bro, you did. But I don't trust this place, so get up with Byrd about it and ask him what's up!"

"Byrd?" Asad repeated his friend's name. "Bro, I had other muthafuckas to handle that type of work," he exclaimed, expressing his disapproval of Fame accepting the hit from Byrd. "Why didn't you? You're right, this ain't the place or time for this conversation. Bro, when the lawyer comes to see you, you need to keep it a hundred with him so he can do his thang. I'll take care of that Asian lady's van you wrecked. Since she's from the hood, it shouldn't be an issue. With that off your plate, all you gotta focus on is proving you acted in self-defense."

"And the peelie?" Fame reminded him when he did not say anything about the stolen car he was driving.

"Say, time's up!" the detective bellowed from the doorway.

"What?" Asad turned toward her at the same time he glanced down at his icy watch.

"Before you go there, I just received a call to move him so you can reschedule this visit with him in the jail."

"Alright, two minutes!" Asad requested.

"You got one!" Tabitha responded as she walked away before he could say another word about it.

"Bro, get up with Slim and give him something to do. He's a good dude to have by your side. You can trust him. I trust him with my life, bro."

"I got you. When the lawyer comes to talk to you, he will have some lines for you to call. You don't gotta worry about shit. I got you," Asad promised before he gave him a lingering fist bump and left the room.

Once in the hall, Asad noticed Detective Allison discussing something with two uniformed MPD officers. When she glanced his way, they locked eyes in a hateful stare for a brief moment, before Asad turned and walked away. The stare lasted a moment too long, because when he turned away, he crashed into Nyte as she was exiting the elevator he was trying to get on.

The collision broke her gold Pandora charm bracelet. Asad was able to catch it before it hit the floor, but not without losing her crushed diamond Hello Kitty charm down the elevator shaft.

"Awww, man! Damn! Why don't you watch where the fuck you're going!" Nyte snapped, snatching her arm and what was left of her bracelet back from him.

"You're right, my bad!" he apologized sincerely.

"You broke it and lost my favorite one," she pouted.

"My bad. I'll pay for it right now," Asad said, removing a wad of cash from his pocket. "How much do I owe you for it?"

"I don't know. The bracelet was a gift, but I bought that charm for $200 myself."

"Look! Here's $500 for your thing, and take down my number so you can call me when you know how much it'll cost to be fixed."

Nyte accepted the cash and stored his number in her phone. Unknown to Asad, Nyte was already thinking of a way to milk him for way more than the bracelet was worth.

"Is everything alright here?" one of the officers asked when walking up on them.

"Yes, everything's fine," Nyte immediately answered. "Don't dodge my call when I call you about this," she said to Asad, waving the fisted bracelet in his face before marching away.

"I got you. Just call," he promised as he got onto the second elevator.

Just before the door closed, Asad saw the beauty talking with the detective. He instantly wondered if they were discussing his brother or him, or maybe it was neither, but these were questions he planned to get answered when she called him.

* * *

Beysik took his eyes away from the afternoon talk show he was watching when he heard his nurse enter the room. She was carrying two plastic clipboards, and he hoped one of them held his discharge papers. He was tired of being laid up in the hospital when his brother and the girls needed him to step up the most.

"Are you here to tell me I can go to the crib?" he asked, muting the TV to hear her answer.

"Oh, I'm sorry. Am I that bad at doing my job that you're rushing to get away from me, Mr. Man?" she playfully pouted.

"Nawl, it ain't you. I ain't even mean it like that. You're cool, Brenda. The doctor told me last night that I should be cleared to leave today, so when I saw you with them clipboards under your arm, I was hoping that one of them is discharge paperwork."

"I'm sorry, but it's not. One is discharge paperwork, just not yours. I'm only here to check on your monitor right now, because some of them have been sending false readings downstairs. So while the techs are on their way here to deal with them, I need to know if there's any more hitches anywhere in our system on every floor," she explained, replacing the playful pout with a look of annoyance. She glanced at the life monitor beside the Beysik's bed.

"Aw nawl! What's that face for? Is mine fucked up?"

"No, it seems to be working fine," she answered before she flipped back a page on one of the clipboards and continue,. "Beysik, my chart says the doctor ordered you another MRI, and it's my guess that your discharge will depend on the results of that scan. I have some bad news for you if that is the case."

"Nope, I don't want it. You can keep it!" he exclaimed, snatching up his cherry Jell-O cup and filling his mouth with some.

"You don't what?" Nyte asked, entering the room and storming beside the nurse. "Brenda, what's he trying to get out of doing today?" she asked without giving Beysik a chance to talk.

"He's not trying to get out of doing anything. He's just being a brat because he doesn't want to hear that the glitch in the computer system has all MRIs on hold until it's repaired," she answered. Nyte then turned back toward Beysik. "That's right, Beysik, you're stuck here with us for at least another day, and that's only if your scan is fine."

"Aww, man! I made plans for us for the day. I brought clothes for him to leave in and everything. Can I take him home and just bring him back in tomorrow?" Nyte suggested to the nurse.

"I'm sure the doctor wouldn't sign off on that. If he was to get hurt or reinjure himself between now and then, the hospital would be at fault," she explained. "But if the techs can get things back up and running within the next few hours, I'll be sure to come take him down for the scan myself so you can keep your plans. But the techs aren't here yet, so, to be honest, the chance of that happening is doubtful."

"Well, since I ain't going nowhere, can I trade in this Jell-O for some ice cream, please?" Beysik requested, lowering the bed from its upright position with the remote. "Sure, I'll bring it right back in as soon as I'm done with my system check next door," Brenda promised.

She then finished writing down the information that she came for, before leaving and closing the door behind her.

"What's that for?" Beysik asked his sexy and scantily dressed girlfriend, who was clutching a wad of cash in her had. "Nyte, don't let me find out that you're up in here bustin' moves on these lames in the elevator," he wise cracked, smiling while checking out her long inviting legs as she sat with them crossed in the chair beside the bed.

"Now you know if a bitch could, she would, but no. This here is just the start of something new." She grinned. "This dude wasn't watching where he was going, and he ran into me as I was getting off of the elevator just now," Nyte explained while taking off her booties with her free hand to wiggle her toes and relax her feet.

"Why did he pay you for bumping into you? Is that some new space age shit that started since I've been in here or some shit?"

"I wish. No, he didn't pay me for that. He paid me because his ass broke my bracelet and lost one of the charms down the opening in the floor between the elevator and the hallway," she explained as she displayed the damaged bracelet that she still had in her hand.

"Hand it here. I think I can fix it for you right now," he said. She passed it to him, which is when he noticed which charm was missing. "Don't tell me the punk made you lose your Hello Kitty?" he asked as he went to work unbending and reconnecting the mangled ring clasp, all the while listening to her tell him what scheme she had in store for her new mark. "Did you get his name?"

"Yeah, he put it in my phone. I didn't really look at it yet." She picked up her phone from beside her purse on the table and pulled up her contact list for Beysik and showed it to him. "Do you know him?"

"I know an Asad, but I don't know if it's the same person. Is he black? If he is, then that fool's holdin'. He's fucks with Jasso."

"Yeah, he's brown skinned, and about your height, I guess."

"Sounds like him, but I don't know for sure. Like I said, Asad's paper is long as train smoke," Beysik said, repeating the phrase that his father used to say. "His team got the whole uptown on lock and most of the southeast side. Ma, before you hit his pockets too hard, let me see who he is. I might need to fuck with him one day."

"Okay, what I'ma do is call him to pay for that, and when he shows up to give me the money, I'll snap a pic of him and send it to you. If it's your guy, I'll let him off the hook; but if not, then I'ma do what I do."

The nurse returned as promised with the ice cream. She brought extra because of the bad news she had about the MRI scan Beysik was hoping to get so he could go home. When she had gone from the room, Beysik was in a foul mood about not being discharged from the hospital. He thought about just walking out, but he knew Noeekwol would be very upset when he found out, especially with how much money he was paying for Beysik's care.

"Oh, thanks, bae! You fixed it!" Nyte exclaimed excitedly.

Beysik fastened the bracelet where it belonged on her wrist. She kissed the corner of his mouth full of gratitude. She then checked the time to see how long she had before the meeting she had requested with Detective Allison.

"It'll hold for now, but sooner or later you'll have to replace that clasp link or it will break again," he murmured, picking up the cup of strawberry ice cream and settling back into bed.

"Bey, don't be all grumpy. You'll be home by this time tomorrow. This hospital can't just let that MRI thing stay broken. I'm sure they need it for more people than just you," she said while rubbing his thigh with a sudden mischievous smile on her lips.

"I bet that bitch could've just taken me down to use one on another floor. This place is way too fucking big to only have one of them machines," he vented before he looked at Nyte's expression. "What are you smiling about?"

"Ummm, let me give you a taste of what I got planned for you when I get you back home."

Nyte did not wait for his answer. Dragging her half inch red fingernails up his body, she slipped her delicate hand beneath the sheets and inside of his hospital gown. At the same time, she climbed into the bed with him. Beysik was instantly aroused by her boldness and the feeling of her straddling him. He had been fantasizing about getting between her legs again more and more since the doctor told him he was going to be discharged.

The delicious feeling of her soft hand massaging his length while she sucked on his neck made his hips move involuntarily. He gripped her soft ass as she continued to work his hardness faster and faster, while simultaneously kissing her way down his exposed chest. She did not stop her descent until her lips were pursed firmly around his tip, working in union with her hand job. Nyte was very talented with her head game, but Beysik wanted and needed to bury his throbbing length into the depth of her warm wet box.

"Get up and gimme that pussy!" he demanded weakly, attempting to pry her mouth off of him.

"Only if you promise to let me do all the work. I don't want you to hurt yourself because of me and have to stay in here longer," she bargained while continuing to manipulate his thickness with her tight fist.

From the way her touch had him sawing in and out of her hand, he knew he was not going to be able to comply with her request. Nyte must have known it as well, because lustfully she went right back to sucking on him. She gave him her throat every now and then, until Beysik filled her mouth with his growing release. She swallowed every last drop.

"That's all you're getting for now, so eat your ice cream so you can cool down," Nyte ordered before getting off of the bed and going into the bathroom to get herself together.

When she returned holding a soapy washcloth to clean up Beysik, Nyte found a nurse in the room with a knowing grin on her face and Beysik pretending to be asleep.

TEN

FROM ALL OF HER YEARS working in the Department of Corrections, the wise security director knew the bangers currently housed in the general population often wanted revenge for what had happened to their cronies on the receiving unit. Lawson also knew that Noeekwol would not want to be placed in protective custody. So her only way to help the champ stay safe was to place him in a single cell.

Once on his new cell block, Noeekwol promptly learned a number of things about DCI's general population. First, the inmate gossip system, known as inmate.com, had already spread the word about him remaining at the prison. It had also spread the word about what he had done to the guys when he was in the dungeon. The second thing he learned was that the daily schedule of the joint barely ever changed. Every day, the champ could count on things happening in a specific order.

At 5:30 a.m., the cell doors were unlocked for the inmate cooks and other kitchen workers to go to work at the main kitchen. Their job was to prepare breakfast for the entire prison.

By 6:40 a.m., breakfast was served down in the main chow hall for the GP inmates, and afterward to the men on the intake units who were fed in the same chow hall.

At about 7:40 a.m., a formal standing head count was conducted. All non-inmate workers were required to stand silently outside of their assigned cell doors until the officer counting them passed by. Then and only then were they allowed back inside their cells, where they remained until count was cleared by control. Once cleared, Noeekwol was free to move about the prison to places such as the library, the hobby room, and the unit's dayroom.

At 12:00 p.m., lunch was served in the main chow hall. After lunch, at approximately 12:40 p.m., there was another standing count conducted the same as before. And just like before, when everyone was cleared, the prisoners were free to move around until shift change.

All shifts changed at 2:30 p.m. During this time, the prison was locked down for about fifteen minutes or so to give the officers time to get themselves situated.

Then at 5:10 p.m., dinner was served until 5:55 p.m., when another standing count was performed. This count always cleared about 6:00 p.m., and all of the GP inmates were then given recreation until 8:00 p.m.

Recreation was held either inside or outside, weather permitting. Outside recreation was in a large, enclosed, mostly grass rectangle yard, surrounded by a high wall and two fully loaded gun towers. Inside the grassy rectangle were a number of activity areas, including a sand volleyball pit, a large blacktop area with three basketball half courts, and a small fitness square containing two pull up bars, two dip bars, and a push up rack. Across from it was a softball field complete with bleachers, so the inmates could sit and cheer on their fellow inmates.

Inside recreation was held in the gymnasium. The gym was a pretty fair size, large enough to run a full court basketball game on two of its six rims or two half court games, and still enough room for the volleyball net to be set up on the far half of the court. In the back of the gym was a cramped weight room filled with just enough weight machines to keep the men happy and in shape. There were no free weights allowed in the prison for fear of the inmates using the bars and plates as weapons.

Noeekwol's first day of outside rec was where he reunited with Vet, but it was in the gym where they both had their first encounters with the leaders of the two most dominant gangs in the prison: the Lords and Disciples. The spokesman for the Lords was a tall, very muscular, and very dark skinned black man named House.

The other man was a six foot two, pit bull faced, caramel complexion man named Flip G, who was the spokesman for the Disciples and friend of the men that Vet and Noeekwol had sent to the hospital from their stay in the dungeon. So the Disciples were out for revenge.

ELEVEN

NOEEKWOL'S DAY HAD STARTED out pretty good, even though it was storming outside. The rain was coming down so hard he could barely see out his cell's window. This was alright with him, because he had been anxious to get into the weight room ever since he had been released from the Box a few days prior. So with no place to go, the champ sat in his cell with his headphones on, jamming out to an old school rap mix countdown as he responded to Heaven's twenty-one questions.

Beautiful,

It's raining like a muthafucka up here right now, so I'm just sitting here with you on my mind. Hey, they just slid a letter from you into my door. It's your questions and some sexy ass photos of you. Damn, girl! I'm missing you like crazy right now. If I wasn't going to work out in a bit, I'd be more tempted to get personal with this hard on I'm holding for you. LOL!

I better clear that up and tell you that I'm in a single cell alone, so don't go there with them crazy ass thoughts of yours. You know what, Heaven, I'm just going to shut up and answer your letter now.

1. *What are the two biggest lessons that you've learned from your previous relationships?*
    A: To be honest, my career as a fighter took up most of my time, so I've never really had a relationship like that. But just to say something, #1 is that it's okay to open up, and #2 is to keep my eyes open at all times like I do in the ring.
2. *What did you learn a little too late?*
    A: That you're special. I wish I'd taken the time to get to know you better sooner, so we would've had more time together.
3. *What things are you too hard on yourself for?*
    A: My training and, more so, for not being home for my mom and dad when they needed me most.
4. *What do most people overestimate or underestimate about you?*
    A: I don't know. You have to ask them.
5. *What do you love about me?*
    A: So far, everything you've shown me. It's like you were made for me.

6. *What is something you probably should do but never will?*

   A: Take a dance class. LOL!

7. *What was the best mistake you've made? What mistake turned out really good?*

   A: Rushing in too hard in that last fight. I was running off of anger, and he could've knocked me the fuck out.

8. *What makes you nervous?*

   A: Judges, police, and dogs. IDK!

9. *What was the last thing that made you cry?*

   A: Seeing Beysik lying in a pool of his own blood.

10. *Do you trust anyone with your life?*

    A: Yes, because being in here I have to.

11. *Do you really believe in love?*

    A: Yes!

12. *What is something that you're embarrassed that you're good at?*

    A: Braiding hair. My lil' sisters made me learn.

13. *Who is the last person that you kissed?*

    A: Really? You know it's you, crazy! LOL!

14. *What should I know about you that I would never think to ask?*

A: That I fight because I hate my relationship with my dad. It's silly now, because I'd give anything for it back right now.

15. Have you ever had a secret admirer?

A: Yeah, you!

16. Have you ever given up on someone but then gone back to them for another round?

A: No!

17. Would you kiss the last person that you kissed again?

A: Yes, I'd kiss every inch of you all over again and again.

18. What is your favorite part of a woman's body?

A: I like nice strong arms.

19. Name five people whose hearts you've broken and why?

A: All of you, and because I'm in here.

20. What is your kindest memory of your mom and dad?

A: My mom and dad.

21. Do you really believe I love you the way I say I do?

A: I believe you feel some part of love for me, but time will tell what part and how much you really do.

Now, Heaven, it's my turn. I expect the same honesty when you answer my twenty-one questions. I'm going to get ready for count now, and then I'm going to the gym. So the whole time I'm working out, I'm going to be thinking of my list for you.
So until then, I'm missing you.
Always,
Noeekwol Bondz

The champ finished his letter just in time for the standing count. When he was allowed back into his cell, he quickly changed into his workout gear of dark gray sweats and black, gray, and white Nike cross trainers. Once count cleared, Noeekwol made sure to grab his black workout leather gloves before joining the others in line at the gate waiting for the call to go to rec.

"Upper and lower tiers, rec!" the officer announced loudly from the unit's entrance, before stepping aside so he would not be run over by the stampede of rushing convicts trying to get to the gym.

Noeekwol caught a glimpse of Vet out in the corridor just before he turned into the gym. Seeing his partner made the champ pick up his pace to catch up to him. He immediately spotted

Vet through the door standing beside an open chest press station. He was watching a group of guys huddled in the middle of the basketball court. Noeekwol paid the men on the court no mind as he made his way over to his friend.

"What it do?" he greeted Vet. "I see you rushed in here."

"Yeah, I saw you, too, and hurried to get here. I just guessed that you might wanna do chest, so I held it down for us," Vet explained as they bumped fists.

"Good guess. I see now why muthafuckas be rushing outta the unit like they do. It's small as hell up in here," Noeekwol said, setting the weight to do a light set just to warm up. "Have you been in the other weight room I keep hearing about yet?"

"Yeah, once. It's way better, but they don't let us use it much for some reason," Vet answered, waiting for his turn on the weights. "Man, bro, put some weight on there. I came to get buff!" he exclaimed, flexing his small biceps in an Ironman pose.

"I am, but not warming up is how you get hurt. We gonna do two sets here and then move up two plates every set until we hit the bottom."

"I can't do the bottom. My max is like 160, but I'll try if you help me."

"I got you, but we ain't gotta rush. As long as you keep showing up for the workouts, you're gonna get there is no time."

"Aye, yo, Bondz! I've been looking to holla at you."

The champ heard the unfamiliar voice boom from the court and turned around. He saw three of the men from the huddle approaching him, and from the hard scowls the two goons flanking the guy in the middle wore, Noeekwol had a good idea who had spoken.

"Do I know you?" Noeekwol asked, taking a few steps forward to give himself some space in case he had to fight.

"Nawl, you don't know me, but I heard you're the one who put my fam in the hospital, and for that we need to holla. Feel me?"

"Look, dude, I don't know what you're on, but I'm trying to work out," Champ said, dismissing him before he turned and headed back to the machine.

"Hey, don't no muthafucka walk away from me until I say I'm done talking to 'em!"

With that said, one of the goons grabbed at Noeekwol's arm and found out that was a big mistake. Noeekwol swiftly clasped him by the wrist and twisted while simultaneously sweeping him off of his feet and sending him crashing to the floor.

"Hell yeah! This is the workout I like!" Noeekwol growled, facing the boss man and very aware of the second group of men quickly approaching from the other end of the gymnasium.

"Yo, fam, leave 'em alone!" the big man said from the other group as he stepped in between Noeekwol, Vet, and the Disciples.

"House, this ain't got shit to do with y'all."

"That's one of mine, Flip, and if the champ's with him, then he's with us!" House told Flip after getting in his face.

The two gang bosses stood eyeing each other with fists clenched for a few long moments. When the officers walked out of their office to see what was going on, Flip instantly backed down, giving both Noeekwol and House a contemptuous chuckle as he backed away.

"Bondz, there ain't no rush. You ain't going nowhere, so we'll be seeing you again real soon," Flip promised, scooping up the basketball as he and his goons walked away.

"That's good looking, homie, but I was good," Noeekwol said to House.

"Bondz, these are my guys. They're cool," Vet spoke up.

"Like he said, Champ, we cool! Looks like since I know y'all are trying to get your workouts on, we gonna go and leave y'all to it. But I think we should really get together and talk soon. I'm a fan of yours. Hell, we all are!" House admitted with a smile. "Flip and them fools didn't know what they were about to get into with you. His silly ass might think he still got it from his high school wrestling days." They laughed in unison.

"That's funny," Noeekwol agreed.

"Yeah, but I'm serious, Champ. Muthafuckas heard you got the title and some wanna see if you deserve it."

"Yeah? What about you? Do you wanna find out?"

"Whoa, I don't know where you're going with that question, so check it. Fall back to the end of the line at lunch tomorrow so you can sit at my table. We can talk then. Cool?"

"It's good. Yeah," Noeekwol agreed before he shook his hand and they parted ways.

When the champ sat down on the bench, he took a scan of the gym and saw that Flip had a

lot more goons with him than when he approached. Seeing that made him more thankful that
House and his guys had stepped in when they
did. Noeekwol also noticed that there were a lot
more Lords in the gym than Disciples at the
time, which gave him an understanding of why
Flip really fell back.

"Vet, do you sit with your guys?"

"Yeah, I'll be over there, but not at House's
table. He has to invite you to sit with him, or you
can't."

"And the guards don't say shit about that?"

"Champ, the authorities know who really
runs this joint. Without the help of the heads and
the OGs, this place would be hell for them to
hold down. And House, he's for real. You should
go and holla at him."

"I intend to, and you're coming with me. I
need them to know that no matter what, I got
your back," Noeekwol said as he finished
banging out the rest of his sets on the chest
press.

TWELVE

NYTE WALKED INTO THE house and found Heaven still in the shower. She was not in a rush to leave, because she was almost an hour early for her meeting with the detective. Nyte saw that Heaven's laptop was on the table, so she decided to use it to check her social media pages while she waited. When she picked it up, she found that Heaven had been drafting a letter to Noeekwol, and she could not help but be nosy. It read:

Noe,

Hey, baby, I'm feeling good but sad all at the same damn time. Well, I've been drinking a lot! LOL! Now I'm all into my feelings, so this letter may sound crazy. I really don't know, but now I'm sitting outside by the fire pit wrapped up in my blanket thinking about you while listening to some old school slow jams.

I'm crying and crying, and wishing we were sitting here together enjoying this nice weather and nice night. I could be wrapped up in your warm arms, but yet I am alone all emotional and horny as hell.

I just want to feel you deep inside me. I crave the feeling of you on top of me. I want to make love tonight, not fuck. But I want to get fucked hard while making love. I want to rub my passion up and down on your face. My mouth wants to do naughty things to you. I want to undress you, touch you, kiss and taste you. I want you hard and hot and deep and fast, and then I want you slow and sweet. I want you under me and on top of me, and sitting and standing. I want to see your eyes when pleasure makes you light up. I want to hold you when you come down and try to find your breath. I want everything with you.

Let me tell you this. Hearing you moan because of me is the sexiest sound ever. I kinda sorta wish I was choking on your dick right now. LOL! But I'm very serious about what I am saying, because being in love with you and not being able to see you every day is hell. Noe, there are times when I'd give anything just to gaze into your eyes or hold you in my arms, if even for a few minutes. I always feel incomplete, like a part of me is missing.

"Can we say nosy?" Heaven exclaimed when she walked into the room and found Nyte reading her letter.

"Girl, you just answered my number one question. Is it just Bey with that magic stick, or do Noeekwol got it too? Now after reading this, I know he do. Shit! Reading this is like reading my own mind!"

"Yeah, whatever! I was drunk," Heaven said, snatching the laptop out of her hand.

"You know drinks are the most truthful, because they're fearless when they do shit. Bitch, it's okay to be a little dick whipped," she teased, and then laughed at Heaven's embarrassment.

"Don't you got some place to be?" Heaven said, rolling her eyes before she smiled.

"Yeah, I'm on it! You just get up with Honey and find out what you can about Rich's thieving ass. We are going to need all the proof we can get if we gonna tell Bey about him, or his ass is gonna try and make it look like we're lying on him."

"Nyte, I don't care what Rich says. Beysik is still going to believe us over him, especially you."

"Let's just be safe," Nyte said as she went into the kitchen to get something to drink.

* * *

The area around 5th and Garfield Street nightclub was filled with families and friends wandering through the crowded residential blocks. Swarms of young, smiling faces went from food stands to game booths and back again. They were all enjoying the annual Garfield Day Celebration hosted by the nightclub owners in the area.

Detective Allison and her friend Aurora vivaciously stood behind a booming wall of large black concert speakers, which were under the shade of the DJ's white and green striped canopy. They were right where she had requested the detective to meet her on the previous day, but they ended up rescheduling to deal with an incident with one of the girls at the brothel.

"Tabi, do we gotta leave right away when you're done with your meeting?" Aurora inquired while ogling the row of hot, delicious smelling barbecue grills and one of the cooks, who was all smiles as he added sauce to a slab of his mouthwatering ribs.

"No, girl, we're not going anywhere before we sample all of this good food out here. To be honest, Aurora, it's the only reason I didn't mind her rescheduling our meeting. It's my day off, and I'm letting my hair down," she answered, scanning the surrounding crowd's faces for Nyte.

"Yeah, let it down then! It's about time you had some fun!" Aurora exclaimed with a big smile on her glossy Mac lips. "You know, I'd almost forgotten about this event.

"Yeah, it's been so long since the last time we've been here," Tabitha agreed, returning a smile to the tall, strong, handsome Latino carrying a full keg of apple flavored beer to one of the stands nearby.

"This used to be your and Bret's spot. Do you think he will show up down here?" she asked, not missing the way the detective was checking out the handsome bartender with lust in her eyes.

"Girl, he has a boyfriend and a doggy now. Remember what brought you down here with me?"

"Yeah, you know I do. But that has nothing to do with you wanting to see his fine ass again. And I wouldn't be a good friend if I did not check in with your feelings every once and awhile, or if I didn't encourage you to give that guy your number. Yeah, I see you!" she giggled. "Speaking of fine, here comes your girl now."

Tabitha followed Aurora's eyes in the direction of the approaching new confidential informant. The first thing that caught their attention when they spotted Nyte was the way she was dressed. The cocoa beauty was dressed in a casual, beige, fitted, cotton Miu Miu wraparound mini dress, matching leather briefs, sheer tights, and Jimmy Choo stiletto booties. Nyte's rose gold and white diamond earrings, bracelets, and rings set the outfit all the way off.

Both men's and women's heads turned as she marched their way. Aurora was caught up in the skilled seductress's seductive glow. She wondered if Nyte always dressed the way she was dressed now, or if she was running off to some scandalous rendezvous after she was done chatting with the detective. Aurora also wondered if Nyte tasted as good as she looked.

Tabitha removed her chrome studded Dolce & Gabbana shades and put on her best greedy smile while waving Nyte over to them. She asked Aurora to give the two of them some privacy to talk once Nyte made it over to her.

"You didn't have too long of a wait did you?" Nyte greeted the detective with a phony friendly half hug and air kiss. She wanted to give anyone who may see them together the idea that they were friends out and about and nothing more. "Ooooh, for Ms. Thang not to be your partner, you two sure do spend a lot of time together," she said, watching Aurora watching her, while waiting on the server to make her a plate. "From the way she's looking at me, I'm starting to think your girl is thinking about adding me to that plate," Nyte said as she winked at Aurora.

"Nooo, I think you're seeing what you want to see. Aurora and I are just friends."

Tabitha could not help but blush a little from the memory of the one time when she and Aurora were drunk on spring break years ago.

"Detective, you know it's my job to know when someone wants me, and your girl is ripe for the picking."

"Sorry, Nyte, but she doesn't pay for sex and she's married."

"Married? Good!" she smiled. "Only a thirsty fool would charge a detective's friend for some fun. She's sexy as hell, and it's been a while since I had me some girl time."

"How about we get down to business and you tell me what you have for me," Tabitha suggested, changing subjects and not wanting to admit that Nyte might be on point about her friend.

"I have some info about Mercy's and Mama's murders, but you're going to have to promise to keep me and Beysik all the way out of it. I'm being real. I need you to promise me that, because these are some really bad men, Detective."

"I can do that if what you have for me pans out. But you're going to have to give me more than just some really bad men." She lowered her voice as a small group of individuals walked by. "Come on! Give me something I can take back to my boss, so I can get this done for all of us."

"Here's what I got for you. But just so you know, I'm recording this, detective Tabitha Allison."

Nyte flashed the screen of her cell phone to show Tabitha that she was not bluffing. She then fed her the story that she made up about the men inside the home of the address she handed to her. Then to really sell Tabitha the story, Nyte agreed to do a ride by with her just to show her exactly where the place was located. Nyte also used the time to lock down a date with Aurora without the detective knowing. She hoped to use Aurora to keep track of Tabitha's movements, just in case she tried to go back on her word.

THIRTEEN

NOEEKWOL WAS SITTING IN his cell reading *Make Every Rep Count*, or MERC for short, to pick up tips for his health and fitness. It was given to him the night before by Officer Buckley. The champ mixed it with tips from the *Men's Fitness Exercise Bible* and formed an exercise routine for him and Vet to do at rec. He was jotting down all of the information so he could give a copy to his partner, when he heard the officer announce that it was time for chow.

Noeekwol slipped on his shoes and his green state shirt. He made sure it was tucked into his pants as required before leaving the cell block, except for when they were going to and from rec. The champ exited his cell and joined the others in the lunch line. Just like House had asked him to, Noeekwol fell back behind the last man in line.

"Aye, yo, Champ? Slow up!" Vet shouted, speed walking up the hall to catch up with him.

"Man, you mean all this time we could've been meeting up like this for chow and you didn't tell me?"

"I thought you knew that my block always got called to chow after yours. My bad."

"Yeah, it is. Got me sitting with these randoms that don't believe in toothpaste. And what in the hell is a chomo?" Noeekwol inquired, leading the way to the chow hall.

"A chomo is a child molester," Vet answered, amused by his friend's ignorance. "Man, dawg, bro! How you ain't know that shit? What, did somebody call you that shit or something?" he asked, briefly pausing from his hilarity.

"Hell nawl! This gay boy next door to me asked if I knew I'd be sitting at the chomo table when I got back from breakfast this morning. I didn't. Shit! I just sat down where I saw an open seat. Hell! The muthafuckas ain't ever said shit to me, and I don't talk to them. Man, Vet, you gotta remember that this ain't my world," Noeekwol explained as they entered the stairwell. "Anyways, do you know what's for chow?"

"Yep! It's the prison's finest: chicken stir fry with steamed brown rice, chow mein noodles, almost fresh bread, soy sauce, and an orange for your delight," Vet recited, like he had been waiting to be asked for the menu. "Aye, Champ, you already know to pass it this way if you don't want it."

"You got it. The only reason I came down was to holla at your guy House," he admitted. "Is you okay down there on your end?"

"All is well. I ain't had no trouble with nobody or nothing. I know a few of the brothas on the deck, so I'm good."

"Do you got everything you need down there as far as TV, radio, and shit like that?"

"Just my shoes and sweats. My paper ain't as long as yours, where I can get that shit sent up here all at once," Vet admitted. "But my OG said she's working on it."

"Hey, give me your info tonight at rec, and tell her that she can relax on that. I'ma have my girl send you that shit. As a matter of fact, make a list of a few things besides the TV and radio."

"Nawl, I'm cool, Champ. I ain't gonna be able to pay that back."

"I didn't say shit about you paying shit back. I can't be having my partner slumming it in the dat room then coming and hanging out with me. I got you, so just get that info to me."

After receiving their trays, they entered the chow hall and immediately located House seated at a table with one other man.

Approaching the table, the champ observed a few of the other men that he recalled seeing with the boss in the gym. House's goons were all seated at surrounding tables slowly eating with an eye on Vet and Noeekwol as well as everyone else in the hall.

Noeekwol also spotted Flip and his crowd all seated up toward the front far right side of the room.

"What's good, Mighty!" House greeted Vet, giving him a quick handshake. "I'm glad you showed up, Champ."

"I wouldn't want somebody to invite me to eat with them and stand me up, so why do it to you?" Noeekwol retorted. "So now that I'm here, what's up?"

"It's like this, Champ. Them boys are mad about the beating you put on their guys down in the dungeon. Then on top of that, you just treated them in the gym last night. So you can count on them getting at you behind that shit, especially since it happened in front of Flip."

"I know they're feeling some type of way. I ain't sleeping on 'em. Believe that. I'm aware of my surroundings all the time," Noeekwol responded, glancing at Flip's table just to let

House know he had seen his new enemy when he walked in.

"And you're supposed to be. Look, Champ, I knew your pops—RIP! He was one of ours; and since you ain't said shit, I'm guessing you ain't plugged?"

"You guessed right."

"See, it don't really work like that around here. Muthafuckas figure anybody who ain't plugged is fair game or a troublemaker."

"Yeah, but I ain't neither one."

"But you are. Look at what you did last night. There was another way to handle that. See, Champ, there's a lot of shit that'll get you fucked up in the joint. I don't wanna see that happen. That's why you need to get down with us, so we can have your back. You know like we did last night in the gym. I know you're good with your hands, but you can't beat that whole mob. Feel me?"

Noeekwol glanced over at Vet and then back to the boss seated in front of him, and thought about what House had said. He knew the man was right, but he needed to know more about the gold toothed thug before he made any decisions.

"Let me sleep on it, and we can have this conversation again once I have all of my facts together. You say you knew my pops, so you know Mercy Bondz ain't raise no fools," he responded before he got up from the table and left Vet behind to finish the two helpings of food.

* * *

Heaven walked into office that read Members Only. She was all smiles and asked Nyte what she had done since they had split up that morning.

"I went and handled that business with that bitch I told you I was going to. And I got a way to keep us all the way in the loop. But it looks like you got something you need to tell me, right? So what's up?"

"Yeah, I do," Heaven said just as she saw one of the girls lingering around the office door and shut it. "I just dropped off Honey at the crib."

"I know you got more than that!" Nyte murmured, leaning back into her seat.

"Yeah, just let me tell it," Heaven said, dropping down on the corner of the desk and sitting so she was face to face with her friend. She also lowered her voice just in case there was an ear at the door. "You know I'm a lot more street smart then half of these lame ass bitches we got in here, right? So I fed the bitch some shit about Rich trying to fuck on NuNu, and the goofy bitch got mad and told me that Rich got another spot on the side and that he's been making the girls do all these shows behind our backs. Honey said he said that he's sick of being number two, and that he feels disrespected that he has to go through us before he makes a move."

"That nigga is so damn predictable at times. I knew when Noe said that shit that Rich was going to have an issue with it. His dumb ass is out there playing the game all sneaky and shit, while we out here trying to make shit happen to keep this money right."

"I hear you, but what can we do to him right now?"

"We ain't gotta do shit! Bey's gotta go in for another MRI in the morning, I know it's gonna be good. So we just keep letting Rich's ass do what he do until Beysik gets back up on his feet, and then we'll let him handle it," Nyte said, picking up and relighting a half smoked blunt.

FOURTEEN

THE NEXT DAY, HEAVEN grabbed the mail out of the box on her way to get in the car with Nyte. Heaven's excitement doubled when she found a letter from her man in the midst of the junk mail.

"Is that from Noe?"

"Yeah, Nyte, who else is gonna be writing me?" she retorted, ripping open the envelope. "Hey, it's the answers to my twenty-one questions and his questions."

"Bitch, you're such a girl," Nyte teased before she turned up the radio.

Heaven flipped her the middle finger and then sat back and started to read the letter.

21 Questions

1. *How are you feeling at this very moment?*
2. *Do you believe in our hearts' connection?*
3. *Would you believe it if I told you that I keep all of your letters under my mattress, so when I lie down, I'm enveloped in your fragrance?*
4. *Can you believe that I woke up with you on my mind?*

5. *Do you understand what these early morning thoughts of you do to me?*

6. *Do you want me to tell you?*

7. *Can you picture me lying in bed naked thinking of your sexy self while gently long stroking my growing erection?*

8. *Will you take over for me so I can concentrate on remembering the sweetness of your kiss?*

9. *Are you nice and wet the way you get just before my tip parts your warm split?*

10. *Can you picture us melting into each other more and more as I stroke you faster and harder?*

11. *Do you need me too, Heaven?*

12. *Can you remember the feeling of me buried deep inside you?*

13. *Would you believe that I'm so hard right now that it's getting harder and harder not to bust?*

14. *Will you cum for me?*

15. *Is it wrong that I miss the way you mumble and stutter my name just before soaking the sheets?*

16. *Can you feel my release filling you?*

17. *Do you know that no other woman has made me feel the way you do?*

18. *Would you whisper your love for me and send it on a kiss in the wind.*
19. *Will you really be waiting there for me when I get home?*
20. *Can you believe I just made a mess of myself?*
21. *Are you mad about the way I just played your game?*

Beautiful, please don't think that I don't want to know everything about you, as I've memorized every inch of you. It's just that there's a lot of bullshit going on in here right now that I'm focusing on. As soon as I get this in here out of the way, I will be able to think clearer and ask the right questions. But you can continue with yours, and I will keep answering them the best I can.

Now, I've been giving some thought about something you said to me awhile back. I don't want just anybody taking care of my little sisters and brothers. There are some real crazies in the world. So I want you to get with Jake and find a good spot to open your daycare. Yeah, I'll be a silent partner, just the way you and my mother talked about.

So I'ma put up the money for you to get started, and you just do your thang with it. As a matter of fact, I think Nyte will be a better person to take with you to look at a place because Jake will try to get a place that's pretty much readymade, because he don't like taking chances with a lot of money. But I know my mother RIP would want to start from the bottom.

Oh, when you can, I need you to send everything on this list to the person on it. If you can do it online now, knock it outta the way for me, please? When was the last time you checked on Bey? What's up with him and everybody? I will call you later. Yeah, they finally got the phone system fixed in this old ass joint.

Well, that's all I got for now. So until next time,
I'm kissing you.
Noeekwol Bonds

Heaven's sudden scream of joy startled Nyte, causing her to tap the brakes a little too soon on their approach to the stoplight.

"Hoe, what did he say that got you screaming like you're crazy?" Nyte demanded, checking the rearview mirror to make sure the patrol car she had passed had not pulled out on her.

"Noe just said that he wants me to open up a daycare for us," she told her with a big smile.

"Why a daycare?"

"I told him that Mama had told me she was thinking about opening one and letting me run it, because of how good I am with kids. I really didn't believe he was listening to me when I said it. I was just trying to take his mind off of everything fucked up that was going on."

"Is that really what you wanna do?"

"Ummmm, yeah! There's good money in childcare."

"Don't you gotta go to school for it, or is it like babysitting at a house?"

"Yeah, I'll have to take a few classes. I don't mind. I don't got nothing else to do. Hell, you take care of all of the real business around here, and I'm just a sexy ass receptionist."

"And what's wrong with that, Heaven? Hoe, you better get your mind right. We're fuckin' with bosses. Do you think I like doing all that bullshit night in and night out? Hell nawl! A bitch wants better. I want to be doing what I'm doing now, running shit with one dick in my life to please. I ain't gonna lie, Heaven. I was kinda jealous when Mama picked you to work at the house. But then if I could handle all of that damn crying all the time, I would still have my son. Do I look like I like crying, cooking, and cleaning?"

"You got a baby? Wow! How old and where is he?"

"Yeah, I do! I think that lil' boy's about five years old. I don't know. Day one when I pushed him out and he yelled at me, I knew it wasn't gonna work with us, and I gave his ass away," Nyte explained coldly, turning onto the hospital grounds.

They were about ten minutes late for Beysik's scheduled discharge time.

While Nyte was looking for a parking spot, Heaven saw Beysik standing out front of the exit doors talking with his right hand man, Rich, so she instantly alerted Nyte.

"What's he doing here?" Nyte exclaimed, stopping the car in the middle of the lane.

"Bey must've called him to come pick him up because we're late."

"Whatever, hoe," Nyte retorted as she brought the car around and stopped right in front of them. "Or his ass is trying to clean up all that foul shit that his punk ass has been pulling and

talking," she said, tapping the horn while scrutinizing Rich.

They took a moment to watch the two men.
Rich stood facing Beysik and appeared very
animated with whatever he was explaining, or
so the two thought. He was explaining what Rich
felt he needed to explain to get ahead of the
boss. Beysik pretty much just stood there
listening and nodding every now and then to
whatever he was being told. When Heaven had
seen enough, she opened the car door and
called out to Beysik as she stepped out to give
him the front seat and she got in the back.

"Bey, are you coming with us or going with
him?" she shouted to rush him along.

"Here I come," he responded before he said
a few rushed words to Rich and shook his hand.

Beysik then used the ugly hospital cane to
inch his way toward the car.

"Why did you call him to come get you, just
because I was a few minutes late?" Nyte
inquired immediately, before he could get in the
car.

"Nawl, I didn't call him. I thought you sent him
when I ran into Slim in the lobby."

"Why would I do that without telling you
first?"

"Whoa, Nyte! What in the fuck is your problem right now?" Beysik snapped, slamming the door shut. "You're the bitch that's late, so kill all that, or do you got something going on with that nigga that you don't want him to tell me about?"

"No, I don't go backward," she retorted while pulling away from the hospital. Nyte checked herself and continued. "It's not the way you're thinking it is anyway."

"Beysik, we don't trust Rich," Heaven spoke up. "He's been talking shit and acting like he's running shit ever since Noe told him to help us out. All we was trying to figure out is why his sneaky ass was up here trying to talk to you now with his lying ass."

"Okay, nawl! Rich wasn't talking about shit. He wasn't even up there for me. I think he said his BM works there in the kitchen. Now since you bitches are all worked up about him, tell me what in the hell he's been up to so I can check that shit before it gets too far outta hand."

Beysik adjusted the seat to ease the pressure of sitting in the car off his back. Nyte and Heaven filled him in on everything they had been keeping from him while he was in the hospital, because they did not want him worrying about anything except getting better so he could come home.

When they were finished giving Beysik a point by point summary of his most trusted lieutenant's treasonous shenanigans, he instructed the girls to put together a get together for him at his father's club, Members Only. The girls were elated to have him back with them, but at the same time, they were a bit leery of how Beysik might handle his sudden position of power.

"Hey, before we go in, let's go down to J.W. and find you a better cane. Because you can't be a boss with that ugly, cheap shit there," Heaven suggested.

Nyte agreed, and they instantly changed their destination to the Grand Avenue Mall to do some shopping.

FIFTEEN

THE ADDRESS NYTE PROVIDED Tabitha with was located in the secluded old industrial neighborhood of Garfield and 31st Street. The house that the detective had been staking out for the past few days was a plain white and maroonish painted duplex with a decent sized fenced in yard. The house was locked up tight with the help of menacing looking black steel security bars and gates on the doors and windows of both the upper and lower levels of the place. Tabitha realized they were there to keep people out, which made her extra curious of the goings on inside the place.

Now Tabitha, along with a handful of her fellow impatient MPD SWAT team members, waited outside of the home for the go ahead to storm the property. The anxious detective made a note that everything appeared to be quiet inside the home of the alleged murders. But she could see some movement going on inside by the constant shadows that passed by the closed window blinds. Tabitha also noticed a dark gray full size Ford passenger van parked in the back of the driveway in front of a blue Volkswagen Jetta.

Over the past few days, she had observed both vehicles make frequent trips to and from the home with different drivers and passengers. Everything seemed to fit in with the information that Nyte had provided, but the detective had yet to catch a glimpse of the men that her elderly witness had reported seeing at the scene of the Bondz shooting.

Tabitha instantly green lit the team, after she received the text from her captain giving her the permission for which she had been waiting. They quickly but silently moved in and surround-ded the house. As soon as everyone radioed in that they were set, Tabitha gave the order for SWAT to knock down the doors. She followed the heavily armed and trained team dressed in black as they poured through both the front and rear doors of the house.

"Police! Police! Police!" the members of the SWAT team bellowed right away announcing themselves. "Get on the floor! Get on the floor now!" they yelled at everyone in sight.

Pandemonium instantly broke out inside the place. Women started screaming in the midst of the police shouting orders to secure the place. Suddenly out of nowhere, two men armed with

Glocks fired on the police. There was a small firefight that the skilled team won, leaving both men dead, but not before Tabitha took a 12 gauge shotgun blast to the chest from a third gunman. She went down hard, banging her head against the wall. The detective was wearing body armor, so she was dazed but alive.

In the end, Tabitha was responsible for saving twelve young teenage girls and boys, four young adult women, and three trans-genders who were all being held against their will and being forced into prostitution by the man that was killed and arrested. Tabitha was able to receive a hug of gratitude from a few of the children despite her badly bruised ribs, before they all were taken away by the EMT to be properly checked out.

* * *

Nyte hated to have to pull herself away from Beysik, but she needed to follow through with her plan. Getting him to understand why she had to go was not hard, because the powerful pain meds he was on had put him right to sleep.

So now she sat across from Aurora at a table in a classy little restaurant that served international food. Since Nyte was familiar with the restaurant's menu, she ordered for the both of them, and then they sipped on Collezione di Paolo wine while waiting for their meal of grilled scallops and onion soup to arrive.

"I'm happy you called," Aurora said between sips of the chianti.

She was ogling at how pretty her date was in the soft light.

"What made you think I wouldn't?" Nyte flirted.

"I don't know! Nerves, I guess," Aurora admitted, showing her nervousness by smoothing out the taut tablecloth with her free hand. She continued to sip on the wine and study Nyte's flawless skin. "Can I ask you something?"

"If we're here to get to know each other right now, I encourage it, or this will just be awkward." Nyte smiled before taking a sip.

"Did you invite me out tonight as part of your, your work? I mean, are you trying to work me for money?"

"Uhh, wow!" Nyte said as she set down the glass. "I don't believe you understand how what I do works." She snickered. "Aurora, if I could just pick who I wanted to pay me for my time, then I'd be a rich bitch. No, Aurora, you're an attractive woman that I want to know better.

That's it, that's all. I don't get to just be me like the way I am with you right now. Men want a fantasy, so that's the mask I wear for them, and they pay me for it. But with you, tonight is just for fun. You're my fantasy," she said, tapping her passion purple polished nails on the wine glass. "Now, my turn."

"What do you wanna know?"

"Your ring. Does your husband know you're here with me? Hell, does he know you like girls?" Nyte inquired.

"I'm not married. This belonged to my grandmother, and my man is a woman. She should know because we've talked about threesomes. We have a pretty open relation-ship."

"An open relationship?" Nyte repeated, thinking about her relationship with Beysik.

"Who's idea was it, yours or hers?"

"Mine, but it's....! Let me say this first. I like girlie girls, but Tori isn't that anymore."

"I understand. So are you hoping to have one with me and her?" Nyte asked, taking a slow sip from her glass while never breaking eye contact with Aurora.

"No!" she instantly answered. "We aren't even really talking right now."

"Why is that, if you don't mind me asking?"

"I needed to come here to Milwaukee to help Tabi with her thing, and she don't like me being here. So now we have our own thing, because I said fuck it and came here anyway."

"So it's safe to say that you're single right now?"

"Single," Aurora let the word roll off of her tongue a moment. "Maybe just for tonight," she answered flirtatiously.

"I guess that's the attitude to have for what we are doing," Nyte said as she shrugged her shoulders and then ran her long tongue across her upper lip, staring into Aurora's green eyes. "Hope we can make this a night to remember."

"That's my hope too," Aurora concurred, lowering her head to break Nyte's penetrating glare.

"Well in that case, let's get outta here and go have us some fun."

"No! I mean, I really want to eat first. Like I said when we got here, I've never been here but always wanted to try the food. Is that okay?"

Nyte took Aurora's hand and agreed to wait until after their meal, because she needed Aurora to feel that the night was all about her. It was Nyte's way of getting into her head the way she needed to be, so she could use her to keep tabs on Aurora's detective friend, Tabitha.

SIXTEEN

WHEN TABITHA MADE IT home from the hospital, she found the place empty. She wondered where Aurora was, but decided not to try to contact her. The detective knew once she told her friend about her dance with death on the job, she would drop whatever she was doing and hurry to her side. So instead she dropped the Mercy Bondz FBI case file onto the oblong glass and polished iron end table, before heading into the kitchen for the half bottle of wine and a big glass, paying no heed to the doctor's instruction about her pain meds and alcohol.

Then she returned to the sofa, kicked off her shoes, wiggled out of her jeans, and found herself a nice spot on the plushness of the sofa. The detective was given three weeks off with pay for the few bruised ribs and small bump on the head she received from the shotgun blast. She was not in a rush to do anything at the moment, so she turned on the TV and settled down to catch up with her favorite show, *Grey's Anatomy*.

In front of the TV sound asleep was where Aurora found Tabitha when she came creeping into the house sometime after 3:00 in the morning from her date with Nyte. Aurora immediately noticed Tabitha's bandaged torso because she was lying there only in her bra and panties. Aurora had to restrain herself from waking her up and asking her what had happened to her ribs, but instead she made a mental note to get all of her questions answered before Tabitha rushed off to work in a few hours.

So instead of waking her, Aurora retrieved a blanket and covered her friend with it. When she capped the bottle of wine, she spotted the name on the file folder lying on the table beside the bottle. Aurora's curiosity got the best of her, and she ended up taking the maroon folder into the bedroom with her to read. She undressed while thinking about how good it felt when Nyte had undressed her hours ago. She remembered how her kisses almost instantly caused little quakes to shoot through her body. Aurora almost came again at the memory of Nyte's head pressing down between her creamy thighs.

Aurora shook it off, climbed under the covers, and then picked up the folder. It read that Member's Only night club, which was the same place Nyte had just invited her to, was owned by Mercy Bondz. Bondz was suspected of human sex trafficking underage runaways, money laundering, and murder. The Fed's file was complete with photos of the pimp, each of which had the word Deceased in bold red letters stamped across them. There were also photos of Nyte and Beysik Bondz that made Aurora wonder even more about Nyte's world. She read the notes attached to the photos of the woman with whom she had just experienced some of the best sex she had had in a long time. The pages stated that Nyte was suspected of drug trafficking and prostitution for the deceased pimp and his son. In the file, the Feds admitted not having much more information concerning Beysik Bondz, so they focused on taking down Mercy Bondz in hopes that the pimp would flip and give up the ones who were shipping the young men and women across the borders to him.

This was the first time Aurora thought that Nyte might have been another sex slave for the pimp, and that she did not have a choice in the world that she lived in. Aurora's heart hurt for the woman, so much so that she slammed the file shut and tossed it on the floor beside the bed before burying her head beneath the covers and going to sleep.

SEVENTEEN

"HEAVEN, WHY ARE YOU over here being all loud and annoying, like you gone crazy?" Nyte exclaimed, irritated and hungover from her night at the club.

"Whatever, blackie," she retorted. "I think I found my building," Heaven told them, ignoring Nyte's moodiness. "I found the perfect building for the daycare center. Here, check it out."

She shoved her Mac Notebook into Beysik's hands, so they both could view the place she was raving about online.

"Oooh, yeah! That's nice," Nyte concurred, taking a seat on the sofa. "Beysik, can you go with me for the open house walk through? I already called and he said he can show it to me today."

"Nope, I can't do it today unless they're willing to show it after about 6:00 or 7:00 p.m. I'm getting ready to go handle something with Rich."

"With Rich?" Heaven repeated with a questioning frown on her face now.

"Yeah, before I put him in his place, I need to know what all exactly that the nigga's been up to. When I'm done with him, I got physical therapy and then I gotta run down to the spot in Racine so I can get this ball rolling the way I need it to be for us," Beysik explained his reasons for declining.

"Oh, I see how it is, bitch! It was just you and me until the world blows up, but now that Bey's back up on his feet, you don't need a bitch no more!" Nyte pouted.

"Nyte, you know it ain't even like that. I was just thinking if Bey went with me, then he can make 'em get straight to business without all of the bullshit. Plus, I know you're coming anyway, so why ask, especially if he does," Heaven explained, unable to contain her excitement.

"You don't know me!" Nyte retorted with a smile before throwing a soft pillow at her.

"Stop throwing stuff!" Heaven exclaimed, tossing it back at her.

"So are you coming or what?"

"Now since you asked him first, the only way I'm going with you is if I can get a job in that bitch when you open it!"

"You know you got that, but what changed your mind?"

"Nothing changed it. I don't wanna have to fuck with them bad ass kids directly. I'm a need something like a receptionist job," she continued to bargain with Heaven.

"Hell, bitch! You can be my assistant director. That way, you can help me keep the girls I hire in check."

"That's what she do best!" Beysik butted in, looking up from his phone and laughing.

"Yeah, I do, don't I?" Nyte smiled. "Heaven, you got a deal. I'm in," she agreed, receiving a sudden hug from her excited friend.

"Now go get ready. I'ma call him back and set it up for like 11:00," Heaven informed her. Then she immediately got on the phone to get the viewing set up.

* * *

The late Mercy Bondz's gleaming pearl white Mercedes S500 pulled up outside the parking structure of the Mayfair Mall. Beysik stepped out of the car to stretch and look around for Rich. The tall thug was leaning on the hood of his black Dodge Charger talking on the phone until he saw Beysik. Rich then hurriedly ended the call and looked over at his boss. Rich saw a small group of teens checking out his car and armed its alarm before joining Beysik in his Mercedes.

"Man, bro, I don't give a fuck what she has going on. You need to get on her so I can get this shit done!" Beysik said, staring heatedly at his right hand man, who sat uncomfortably in the passenger seat.

"B, I'm telling you that bitch won't do it. I've been at her about it, and she ain't going!" Rich explained, a little agitated by Beysik pressing him to make Honey do something when she was mad at him about the text messages she had found on his phone just before the meeting with Beysik.

"Check this, bro! I know she's your bitch, but if I say she'll do it, then she's gonna do it!"

"Then your ass needs to holla at her."

"But, bro, you ain't even got to send her on the road. I gotta plug right here. And he got some good work. Why don't you come with me when I go holla at him to cop later?"

"Yeah, I'll do that, but I'ma still set shit up with Honey just in case," Beysik told him, not liking Rich's demeanor.

He could see that Rich had gotten kind of sloppy; and with that, Rich got out and headed back to his car, knowing that there was nothing more to say. Beysik picked up his phone and called Honey like he said he would.

"Hello?" she answered, sounding like she had been sleeping.

"How's my favorite bitch?" Beysik asked her smoothly.

"Psst!" Honey answered, sounding even grouchier.

"With who, me?"

"Bey, you know who!"

Beysik chuckled and cleared his throat before getting down to the reason for his call.

"What's this shit I hear about you not acting right?"

"Don't talk to me like I'm one of them punk hoes!" she retorted.

"Look, I ain't talking to you no kinda way. You ain't mad at me. You're mad at bro. I'm just trying to remind you that good bitches always win in the end."

"I take it that Richard ran his ass over there talking to you?" Honey asked, with her lack of respect for her man clear in her tone of voice.

"He sure did, and he told me you're planning on backing out of taking this trip for me."

"Yep, that's absolutely correct. Fuck that shit! I ain't trying to help him shine for the next bitch when he ain't shit. And I know if I do it for you, then it's gonna be the same as helping him. I should be treated the same way Nyte and ole girl are, so fuck that!"

Beysik took a deep breath to check his irritation. He remembered his pops telling him that keeping calm was necessary in his profession, especially when dealing with another muthafucka's trash.

"Honey, why you pulling something like this when I got my cash already in play?"

"Because."

"I told you a while ago that this was a part of our deal. You can do what you want after you do what's needed for the team. I didn't tell you to start fucking with Rich. That was all you. So don't let that shit fuck with what we got going on."

"Beysik, I'm having a baby now," she confessed. "I can't be up and doing that shit no more."

"Okay, I understand," he said in a calmer voice. "I'll hit your hand with a little something extra for the baby."

"Don't try to pacify me! You can find somebody else to make that move for you. You got Nyte, so you don't need me!"

"Bitch, don't tell me who I need to do shit! I ain't been in the fuckin' hospital that damn long. You know how I get down!" he snapped. "It's best that you remember your place and who you're talking to." He paused for a moment knowing that he should not have yelled at her like that. "My bad, Honey. You're about to be a mother now. I get it. You's a hoe first!"

"Fuck you, Beysik! You can't make me do it. I'm fuckin with a boss just like you now!"

"Oh, are you really? And who might that be?" he asked, but she did not dare answer, knowing that she might have said too much. "I expect you to make that run and do any other task I see fit. And if you don't send the boss of yours to holla at the god, I can send him to holla at God. You seriously should think on that, and let me know by the time that knucklehead little brother of yours gets outta school."

With that, Beysik ended the call.

EIGHTEEN

THE GIRLS PULLED OVER and parked in front of the property in which they were interested. It was located in the middle of the block of Appleton Boulevard and Hampton. Even now in person they both agreed that it was the perfect place for a daycare center. There was a cozy little playground right down the street from the building, plus it was in the middle of two of the city's bus routes. That would make it easier to get to for the mothers who did not drive. Also the surrounding neighborhoods were not bad. So far, the place seemed to be just right. Heaven and Nyte got out and went inside, and there they were met by the seller.

"Good afternoon, ladies. I'm John," he said, offering them a handshake.

"Hi, John, I'm Heaven, the one you spoke to on the phone, and this is my sister, Nyte," she introduced them and shook his hand.

"From our call, I understand that you're wanting to turn this place into a childcare center, right?"

"Yeah, that's right," Heaven responded, observing the red brick trimmed walls and reddish brown granite tiled floors through the entrance lobby.

"Well, I believe this is your place. It's just right for what you are trying to do with it. This place used to be a recording studio. As you see, it has the square footage you need to be comfortable. There's a room up here that can be used as another office space, and three others in back. If you care to follow me, I can show you, because me telling you isn't doing any good," John said, leading the way to the back rooms.

"Yeah, this is nice," Heaven exclaimed as soon as she stepped foot in the space.

"Are all of the rooms this size?" Nyte asked, thinking about how the space could be turned into a classroom or two depending on how big Heaven wanted the class sizes to be.

"More or less, but I intend to let you see every part of the place. Like I said, I think it's just right for your center."

"How long have you been a realtor, John?" Nyte asked, thinking of how bad he was at pitching the place to them.

"Oh, I'm not a realtor. I am the owner. I'm showing the place myself because I want someone to have it who has a dream that they want to bring to life, just the way my daughter had before the big C took her," he answered sincerely.

"Oh, I'm sorry to hear that," Nyte responded just as sincerely, without letting down her guard because of the sob story about his daughter dying.

"I want it!" Heaven whispered to Nyte.

The girls continued to follow John, and Heaven's excitement continued to grow with every step they took while touring the building.

"I like it, too, but you gotta calm you ass down before he tries to tax us for it. It's just like buying a car. We gotta show him that we won't be swindled," Nyte responded to Heaven before she turned to John. "How old is this place? I mean, does it have any major plumbing or wiring issues that we need to know about?"

"No, none of that! My daughter had to have this place completely remodeled to meet her needs, so everything is up to code. I don't know when the building was constructed exactly, but she had it remodeled about seven years ago."

"Okay, so let's talk price. I don't remember seeing one listed on the site," Nyte replied.

"Yeah, we like what we see, but what's ideal may not be a deal or affordable," Heaven added, getting her head in the game now.

"I'm asking $90,000, which is much lower than the market price of $120,000, I believe," he said, giving them his best sales pitch.

When he was done making them the offer, Heaven was the new owner of the building.

Nyte had talked ole John down some more, getting him to lower the price by $20,000 less than the asking price. The skillful, cunning whore used his spiel about his daughter back on him. Nyte pulled the man's heartstrings by telling him that she had just gone through a throat cancer scare herself. She followed that by saying that the scare made her see that life was too short to wait on dreams to happen, when you can use the time to make them happen now. The old man was so emotional when she was done talking that Nyte probably could have gotten the place even cheaper had she pushed.

"I'm glad you were here with me. I wouldn't have ever gotten him to lower his price like that without playing with his old funky ass balls," Heaven joked once they were back in the car.

"Now why do his balls gotta be funky, Heaven?" Nyte laughed. "But I ain't gonna lie. I kinda feel bad about lying to him like that. I was going to talk him down anyway, but not like that."

"Then why'd you do it?"

"I thought he was running game on us about his daughter, because that's the kinda shit you see on TV. But when I said I went through it myself and his eyes teared up, I knew he was being sincere with us about it."

"You know what, bitch? We gotta hurry up and get this place together so we can open, because your ass is getting soft," Heaven teased her. "Fuck his feelings. Since when do a few tears from a john named John make a bitch feel bad. All else aside, girl, what's really on your mind?"

"Honestly, I was just thinking about Bey in there. When he was in the hospital, I didn't know what I was gonna do. I felt like my world was about to end."

"I know just what you're feeling. I felt the same way when all that shit went down. And then on top of that, I had to watch Noe turn himself in," Heaven admitted, taking a breath and shaking off the memory.

"Since we in the car opening up and shit," Nyte said, turning in her seat to face her, "that's why I had an attitude with you that day when

Noe went in. Heaven, I don't think you fully see shit the way I'm seeing it. Them two brothers are our men. They're turning us from hoes to housewives. Right now I'm sitting here wondering if Beysik remembered to take his pain meds and eat something. If that ain't housewifey shit, then what is?"

They continued to vent to one another on their way to do some shopping. Heaven was so eager to tell Noeekwol the news about the building that she had to pull over and let Nyte drive, so she could start drafting the letter to him on her phone.

"Nyte, I think we should name the center Felisha's Blessings after Mama, as a thank you to her for giving us Noe and Beysik."

"Yeah, I like that," she agreed as she turned onto Highway 100 south toward Mayfair Mall.

NINETEEN

APPROXIMATELY 128 HOURS HAD passed since Beysik came home from the hospital. He knew that to be able to take the reins of his father's operation, he needed to power through his pain. So with the addition of the flashy gold Leo headed walking stick Nyte had picked out for him, Beysik slid into the passenger seat of Rich's ruby red Ford Mustang GT.

The young boss was curious to know who Rich had been going through to cop the three kilos of soft white work needed just to keep his small part of Beysik's drug operation going. Beysik could never have an issue with Rich using the money that was left with him to keep shop open. As a true hustler, that is exactly what he was supposed to have done. The girls could not have done it, nor could Noeekwol. They would not even have known where to start. So, no, Beysik's issue was that the money Nyte had given him from what Rich had been turning in to the girls did not add up. Now, sitting in the soft leather seat of Rich's new whip gave him a good idea why.

"B, you sure you're up for this already? I can handle it by myself and reset it up for you to meet another time, so until you're 100 percent on your feet, bro."

"Bro, let's roll. I had enough down time. Now it's time for the boss to boss up and get back at it. If your connect is holding the way you say he is, then I'ma need him to double them three you copping just to see how it does down the way. Plus, it'll show me he can handle my flip. If he can, then I ain't gotta put your bitch on the highway no time soon."

"He got that shit, bro. And don't think I missed that lil' shot you sent at me about me copping three. Come on, now, you know how I get it up, bro. We going in to snatch up five of 'em," Rich boasted, lying about the actual number of bricks he had been getting.

Unknown to Rich, Beysik had reached out to a few of his loyal clients to get an understanding of how Rich had been handling business with them. They immediately asked Beysik when he was bouncing back in the game, and they all stated that Rick had been taxing them as well as giving out garbage dope. Three of Beysik's clients informed him of the amount of kilos they were buying, and collectively just these three were purchasing the five bricks that Rich just claimed to be heading to pick up on the re-up. Beysik had to ask himself how Rich planned on hitting them with what they needed as well as keeping shop open for him.

"Aye, how long have you had this here?" Beysik asked about the car to change the subject. He did not want to let on to what was actually on his mind.

"A lil' more than a month. I just got it from having the rims slapped on that day I ran into you at the hospital and shit," he answered. "Hey, did you holla at them bitches about not telling me what hospital you was in and shit? I would've come and checked on you. But they were being all funny acting and shit."

"I handled that, but what size rims is these, 24s or 6s?"

"Both! I got 24s in front and 6s in the back, so it can sit the way it do and still ride good."

When they arrived at the former furniture store located on the northeast side of the city on the corners of Palmer and North Avenue, Rich had taken him into the heart of the ESG's hood. So the first thing that sparked Beysik's attention was that there was not one of them out on the block. The next was the setup of the meeting place. The parking lot was fenced in, making it one way in and one way out. Beysik was not going to let himself be caught in the death trap.

"Bro, how many times have you met with these muthafuckas here?"

"This the first time. We usually just bust moves in traffic. But Nut had us come down here because this a new batch, and he thought you would wanna come in and check it out first."

"Yeah, I don't like being closed in, so don't park in there. Park on the street. As a matter of fact, I'm not about to do all that walking. My back is fucking with me just sitting, so I'ma chill in the car and let you handle it. I've heard of P-Nut, so I'm sure he knows me, and I know you know what I like. So, yeah, I'ma chill out here," Beysik said while staring out at the building.

"I told him you was coming with me so he wouldn't trip about it, so you good."

"But like you said earlier, I ain't 100 percent, so I can't take no chances down in this hood. Shit, you can see if fam will come out to the car and holla at me."

When Rich got out of the car and went inside, Beysik scrambled over into the driver's seat just in case he needed to make a prompt getaway. He sat and watched Rich disappear through the service door of the building with the money bag. He then took the caution to really scan the area. There was nothing moving in the building's surroundings, which was really strange for the east side of Milwaukee.

Beysik's wait for Rich was not too long. But when he did return to the car, he was empty handed. He explained that he did not like the product because the work was not flaky enough for him. When Beysik inquired about the money, Rich told him that he left it with P-Nut so he could just drop it off to him once he had the product that he was used to getting.

Beysik agreed just to play along, but the whole setup of this so called meeting that Rich was supposed to have put together seemed fishy to him. So for that reason, Beysik would not be accompanying him whenever Rich decided to re-up again later. They traded seats before Rich pulled off. As they rounded the corner, Beysik peeped out several big black tinted out police SUVs trying to look inconspicuous in the ghetto. When Rich did not comment on them acting like he did not see them, the seasoned thug wondered how long his partner had been working for the Feds.

Right then, Mercy Bondz's words popped into his son's head: "If you can't trust 'em, bury 'em. It's always a better one to fill that one's shoes."

TWENTY

WITH HER PAID MEDICAL leave, Tabitha decided to visit her parents who lived in Green Bay,
Wisconsin. She thought that a little traveling
would do her some good, and since Aurora was
not ready to make up with her spouse yet, she
happily house sat for her. Aurora's job as an
insurance adjuster allowed her to work from
home, so doing this for her friend was not putting
her in jeopardy of losing it and becoming
homeless.

Aurora was using Tabitha's desktop computer in the home office to catch up on some
work, when her thoughts went from the task at
hand to ones of what she had read in the file
about Nyte. The last time they were together,
Nyte had offered Aurora to come watch her
work. Just to kill her curiosity about it, as Aurora
really wanted to know what about it made
someone as pretty as Nyte stay.

When she could not stop thinking about the
sexy younger woman, she just stopped fighting
it and picked up the phone.

"I wasn't expecting to hear from you so soon," Nyte lied. "What's up?"

"Nothing much. I'm just sitting here waiting to clock out for the day."

"Oh, so you are at work right now?"

"Yeah, I'm on break," Aurora said, putting her feet up on the desk and smiling. "How about you? Are you working? Do you have a few minutes to talk?"

"Yeah, I can talk. Is something on your mind, or are you just ready for another play night?" Nyte flirted.

"Am I!" she giggled. "Yeah, I'm ready, but that's not the only reason you've been on my mind," Aurora admitted.

"It's not? Then what?"

"Nyte, a few nights ago I read a file that Tabi had on your old boss, Mercy. Oh, is it cool to call him that? Pimp just seems kinda harsh talking to you."

"It's cool, but what about this file made you call me?"

"It was mostly about him, but it mentioned the name of that place you offered to take me to; and, well, I want to take you up on the offer, if it's still open to me."

The phone was quiet for a long while. Aurora was starting to think Nyte had hung up on her and checked the screen.

"So you wanna come in my world of selling sex, huh?" Nyte asked nonchalantly. "Okay, just tell me when a good time for you is, and I will set it up."

"Nyte, you tell me because I want to really see what it's like. I don't want some generic version. I promise you this is for me and not for Tabi. She don't even know about our night together," Aurora confessed, praying that she believed her.

"Girl, I ain't worried about the detective. But I am curious to see what she said about me in that file. There must have been something good to make your sexy ass call me?"

"It's nothing she said. I can bring you a copy of it so you can see for yourself. Nyte, there's something I might wanna talk to you about after you read it," she said, hoping the offer would get Nyte to trust her more.

"Okay, you do that and be ready to watch me do my thang tonight at around 12:30? No! Make it 11:30, so I can give you what you're really looking for and send you back home so you won't be too tired for work in the morning."

Aurora agreed and ended the call. She then logged off of the computer and got right up and copied the FBI file without a second thought about it.

* * *

Heaven and Nyte were wandering through the aisles of Home Depot's paint department. Heaven was looking for fun colors to paint the nursery at the center. While she worked on the color schemes, Nyte played Candy Crush on her phone. She had just cleared level 4 when she received a text from Beysik asking her to call him ASAP. Nyte promptly ended the game and called him.

"Hey, daddy, what's up?"

"Where are you right now?"

"I'm with sis trying to find some paint for the center. Do you need me to come to the house?"

"Nawl, I'm not even in the city right now," he confessed.

"What you mean you're not in the city? Where you at?"

"I'm on my way to Racine to grab something right quick, but check it."

"But check nothing, Bey," she interrupted. "Did you even go to your physical therapy today like you were supposed to?"

"I had it rescheduled for tomorrow because something came up with that problem child again, and I needed to handle this business first. Nyte, I'm good. I got Diesel with me. Now listen."

"Okay, what?" she responded, now irritated a bit by him not taking care of himself first.

"I need you to get up with ole boy that you bumped into at the hospital and arrange for me and him to have a meeting. Do you know who I'm talking about?"

"Yeah, I'm on it. What time do you want it for?"

"Let him pick the time and place. Just try to make it ASAP. Let him know I'm trying to spend this paper with him, and hit me back as soon as you're done."

"Bey, do you just want me to invite him to the party instead of giving him space to turn you down?"

"You can, but I'd rather you let him pick the place so he'll feel comfortable enough to talk. You know what, do both."

"Alright," Nyte agreed, then ended the call and pulled up Asad's phone number from her contact list. She sent him a text asking if he could talk, and if so to call her as soon as he could.

Asad called her back, and after Nyte explained what she wanted, Asad informed her that he was not in town at the moment but would have one of his people meet up with Beysik if that would work for him. Since Beysik had made it sound urgent, she agreed and told Asad to have his people text her the time and place. Nyte ended the call after he accepted her invite to the party at Members Only.

* * *

There was a catch to being housed at DCI. The requirement for the champ to stay in the less populated maximum security prison was that he had to work, or he had to be one of the terminally ill inmates on the prison's hospice unit. Since Noeekwol was in perfect health, he had to find a job. If the champ could not find one on his own, then he would be placed on relief worker detail. Relief detail included all the unscheduled workers that could be called in to any job at any time. Noeekwol was doing his best to avoid being placed on that crew, because it would disrupt his daily workouts.

He was having a hard time finding a job that fit his needs. The Health Services Unit was filled with the white supremacist guys, and they were trying to charge him a monthly fee for the job. The laundry positions were being held down by the Mexican posse, and they were just involved in too much nonsense for him. Pretty much all of the rest of the jobs were the same way or did not fit his schedule.

When House found out about the champ's predicament, he had both Noeekwol and Vet placed in the main kitchen with him and his guys. House got Vet a job on the tray prep crew, where his duties were to prepare trays and deliver them to all of the units that fed their inmates on the cell blocks. House hooked the champ up with the meat man position alongside him. The position's hours were from 6:40 a.m. to about noon, six days a week. Noeekwol's duties were not just to cut meat. He also set up meal carts for the cooks, and he had to stock and inventory all of the freezers and mix and bake the meatloaf.

With Noeekwol's love for fitness, the constant lifting of heavy frozen cases of meat and veggies worked perfectly for him. After working with House for a few days, Noeekwol made the choice to go ahead and clique up with the Lords. He did not do it for protection or power; instead, he joined them to feel closer to his deceased father and to be even closer to Beysik. When House asked the champ what encouraged his decision, all he could think to tell him was that the Almighty was in his blood.

TWENTY - ONE

THE YOUNG HOOD BOSS sat in the back seat of a gunmetal black Chevy Equinox with two of his loyal soldiers. It was one of two that Beysik had Diesel rent for the move that they were about to put down. Besides Diesel, there were three other men with Beysik. In Beysik's SUV were Diesel and QXL. In the other were Hakeem and Corey, who were parked on the opposite end of the block. They were all waiting for the target to come out of the house, because the others inside the home had nothing to do with their loved one's disloyalty.

Beysik wanted to hurry things up so he could get to the party the girls had thrown together for him like he had told them to. The party was partly to show appreciation to all of the team that stayed down when Mercy Bondz was killed, and the other part was so everyone there could be his alibi for what he was about to do.

* * *

Aurora showed up with the copy of the file as promised, and Nyte took her inside of Members

Only so she could witness all of the freaky things the private event had to offer.

"Wow! This is nothing like I imagined it would be!" Aurora yelled over the loud pounding music. "It's like, basically being inside a strip club."

"Look at you!" Nyte said, surprised. "What do you know about strip joints?"

"I've visited one or two in my life." She blushed.

"Well basically it's that and then some. The difference between here and a strip club is that the hoes gotta wait until they're off work and take their dates to a motel. Members Only is a one stop shop. Everything's here!" Nyte explained, taking Aurora's hand and towing her through the maze of tables, at some of which sat rowdy men that copped feels of their asses as they went by. "It's not called Members Only for no reason. To partake in the pleasures, you have to be somebody, except for tonight."

"What's different about tonight?"

"Tonight is a welcome home party for Beysik."

"So it's not going to be authentic then?" Aurora asked with a look of disappointment on her face.

"No, it's going to be live, just the way I promised. See, up here is where these hoes catch their dates. If he or she wants more than a steamy lap dance, then they can get a room downstairs. It's set up for the ones that want to live out their freaky fantasies and to do some fucking and sucking in the process."

"How much are the rooms?"

"Why, do you want to get one with me?" Nyte flirted.

"I'm just curious, but would you really charge me?"

"No hard feelings, Aurora, but work is work and play is play. If you wanna spend time with me in here, it's gonna cost you," Nyte said, and then burst out laughing when she saw the look on her face. "I'm just playing, but it is a house rule."

"Don't do me like that. I really thought you were being serious," she admitted, then smiled. "Now for real, how much are they?"

"It all depends on what you're trying to do. But the rooms are priced from $30 to $100, aside from the price of the escort. They start at $200."

"Wow, $200 an hour?"

"Bitch, please, that's for a nut. It's another price after that first one. I can make a G in 45 minute on a good night."

"Really?"

"Yeah, there's a lot of freaky people in the world," Nyte skillfully lied while paying close attention to Aurora's body language. I see you ogling that hoe on stage. Should I be jealous?"

"Nooo, it's nothing like that!" She was blushing again. "I was just watching her dance."

"You know what? I wanna see you dance," Nyte said, taking her hand and pulling her toward the stage. "Let's get you up there so you can shake it for me."

Aurora stopped in her tracks. When Nyte asked her what was wrong, she told her she did not think she could dance on stage in front of all of the people watching. Nyte tried telling her that dancing on the stage was no different than dancing on the dance floor in a crowd. But Aurora was not trying to hear that. She looked around at all of the girls dancing seductively for their tables. Some of them were dancing or

ASSA RAYMOND BAKER

doing something in dark corners of the club and just could not move.

"Okay, then do you wanna see me do my thang?" Nyte offered.

"Up there or at a table?"

"If I'ma do it, it's gonna be on stage so I can get paid while I'm showing how I can work a pole."

"Yeah, sure. Let me see you work it!" Aurora said, relaxing now that she was not being asked to dance anymore.

"Like I said, if I'ma do it, I'ma do it right. So let's grab something to drink and down us a bunch of Jell-O shots to get in the mood, so we can really get this party started."

* * *

Rich received a text from Diesel asking him where he was. He replied telling him that he was at his mom's crib getting ready to head out to the party. Diesel texted back telling him that he was on his way for a half kilo of hard. That was over thirty minutes ago. Rich got tired of just waiting for him to show, so he called him. Diesel's phone went straight to voicemail repeatedly. He wondered what had happened to him, and guessed from the sudden way his

154

phone went offline that Diesel might have gone to jail on his way to him. So Rich decided to head out to Members Only for a good time.

He was not going for Beysik. Rich was going for Heaven. He thought it would be good to have a real dime in his life, one with no hidden desires. Rich thought he might shoot his shot at her at the party. He even thought of shooting a little cash her way to reel her in. He checked his appearance one last time before walking out of the house to his Dodge Charger. He was standing beside the car texting back and forth with Honey when suddenly a shadowy figure in a hoodie popped up on the opposite side of his car.

"Whoa, whoa! Slow up, homie! Don't move, and let me get all of that shit up off of you!"

Before Rich could react, an unknown truck sped up and slammed to a stop beside him with its trunk popped open. The next thing Rich knew, he was being savagely knocked upside the head from the guy that was behind him and then tossed into the back of the truck unconscious. The man in the hoodie picked up Rich's keys and jumped into the Charger, and then all three vehicles sped away.

About fifteen minutes later, all three vehicles pulled up beside the lagoon on the dark side of Washington Parkway. QXL jumped out of the Charger and immediately trained his gun on the trunk of the Equinox. So when Corey popped it open, Rich found himself staring at the barrel of the goon's Glock, daring him to make any sudden moves.

"Bitch ass nigga, get out!" QXL commanded, twisting the gun eagerly back and forth but keeping it aimed steadily at Rich's face.

"Okay, okay!" Rich retorted, slowly easing out of the rear of the SUV and scanning his surroundings while remembering all of the times he had talked down to the goon holding him at gunpoint.

Rich figured out where he had been taken. At this hour, the park was almost as dark as it was desolate, if it was not for the few sparsely placed lamp posts on the trails.

"Q, what's this about, bro? If it's money, I got you. All you gotta do is take me back to my car," Rich pleaded.

"Thanks for that info. Now you can tell me where the rest of my shit is!" Beysik bellowed, stepping out of the back of his SUV parked by the lagoon.

Before Rich could respond, he was snatched up and half dragged over to him.

"Aye, Self! What do you want us to do with this rat bitch?" Corey asked the young boss.

"B, what the fuck is you doing?" Rich pleaded in shock, "Tell 'em to let me go, and let's talk about whatever it is that's on your mind to have you do me like this."

"Fuck you! Your rat ass gave up your right to work out shit with me the moment you thought you could take my place by setting me up to get knocked with that fake ass buy. Did you really think I would fall for that shit?"

"What, bro? You're tripping, bro, for real! I wouldn't do no rat shit like that to you. Yeah, I did some shit to get a little extra cash, but that's all. Please, Beysik, let me go?"

"Rich, this ain't me trippin'. This is a boss demanding loyalty. If I let one get away with it, then all of y'all might wanna shot at the title. Pop told me not to trust you. His exact words were, 'Never trust a bitch that won't show you his eyes.'"

"B! Wait, man!" Rich exclaimed, taking a shaky sidestep. "You don't gotta do this."

"Diesel, show him what loyalty looks like, and show me that you deserve his spot," Beysik ordered, stepping behind the goon with the gun. "Kill him and toss his ass in with the fish."

At the sound of the kill order, Rich broke free of Corey's grip and spun around to make his escape, just as Diesel's finger was pulling the trigger of his .357 SIG auto. Rich was struck in the shoulder, back, and head. The powerful slugs sent his body crashing and splashing into the lagoon. Then without warning, QXL shot Corey in the face.

"What you shoot him for?" Diesel inquired, with his gun now aimed at QXL.

"He let him go, and I wasn't sure if he did it on purpose. Mercy Bondz once told me that if a muthafucka's actions ain't clear, then neither is his loyalty," the goon answered with his gun at his side.

"Okay, sounds good to me. Get their phones and shit, torch the car, and then meet us at the club," Beysik ordered Hakeem and XXL before climbing into the Equinox with Diesel and fleeing the scene.

TWENTY - TWO

NYTE WONDERED WHERE BEYSIK and the others were when she did not see them socializing anywhere in the club. She then spotted Heaven going into the manager's office with the file she had passed off to a barmaid to pass on to Heaven when she saw her. Nyte smiled, knowing Beysik would be pleased with what she had done. She turned her attention back to Aurora. The 100 proof Jell-O shots she had been feeding her were starting to do their job. Nyte could see Aurora relaxing more and more, so she pulled her into the dressing room to discreetly check her for any type of surveillance device.

Once in the little changing room, Nyte immediately disrobed in front of Aurora. She started dressing in a white and silver angel costume.

"Wow, you look hot! Like a model on a Victoria's Secret runway," Aurora slurred her compliment.

"Thanks, girl, I bet you'd look good in this," Nyte said, pulling out a sexy butterfly costume, complete with knock off red bottom Prada glittering rainbow stilettos, and wings. "I even got a wig that you can put on so nobody will ever know it was you on stage."

"Hey, I've been looking for you two!" Heaven announced when she entered the room. Nyte could see that Heaven was also a little tipsy.

"Oooh, yeeess, with that ass and them big ole titties, girl, you're gonna have 'em howling like fools and praising your name out there," she said, looking at the outfit Nyte was holding up for Aurora. "When you bounce that ass, they gonna make it rain for you, girl!" Heaven encouraged her.

"I don't know about that!" Aurora responded, looking a little nervous again. "I can't wear that. It's pretty and all, but I don't have that young tight body anymore that you two have. I'm gonna need to do a couple hundred sit-ups before I can even think about putting on that little two piece."

"Oh no, girl! You're being too fuckin' hard on yourself. You're good, I promise you that. Aurora you have nothing to be ashamed about with that body of yours. If I like it, then that bunch out there will 1ove it," Nyte told her.

"Oh, okay! Fuck it! You know what?" Heaven exclaimed. "Fuck this shit! I'll wear it. We're here to have fun tonight, right? And, Nyte, you said you're giving Ms. Thang here an all-inclusive experience, right?"

"Yeah, that's what I said," Nyte retorted, surprised by Heaven coming out of retirement.

"Okay, so let me get that and give her—!" Heaven quickly searched through the outfits that were left. "Give her this black studded one piece," she said, then plucked the angel outfit from Nyte's fingers and started undressing and shamelessly redressing into it in front of Aurora.

"Okay! Alright, alright! Give it here, but I'm only getting on stage," Aurora told them, giving in to their peer pressure. "Do I still get a wig with that one?" she inquired, checking out the black leather dominatrix costume with tall black silver studded, platform thigh high boots.

"Yep, you can choose any color you want," Nyte answered with excited approval, while smiling as she helped Aurora disrobe.

* * *

Beysik was decked out in Louis Vuitton from head to toe, and he complemented the outfit while paying homage to his father by wearing the late Mercy Bondz's signature big gold icy crown link necklace and pendant. Beysik and his new lieutenant, Diesel, entered the club through the rear door, blending right in with the crowd. After making a few rounds, they split up at the bar. Beysik was impressed with the way Nyte and Heaven had put the event together for him. The young boo grabbed the triple shot of Patrón from his sexy barmaid, while promising himself that he would make his dad proud by keeping everything moving forward. He also made a mental note to keep Nyte in charge of this part of the operation. She was his woman, so that made her the HBIC, and he planned to make sure everyone respected her as that from there on out.

Beysik briefly looked around for the girls, and when he did not see them right away, he went into the office and sat down with the FBI file copy. The file described in some handwritten notes what the Feds knew about the deceased pimp's business dealings. Beysik smiled even bigger when he saw that there was no mention of Noeekwol at all as part of the family business, and he planned on keeping it that way.

However, there were a lot of photos of people that Beysik needed to know, as his father had done business with them in the past. Asad and Jasso were among the listed names and photos. Tears welled up in his eyes when he came across the crime scene photos of his parents slumped over and murdered inside of his father's Escalade. Beysik kissed the photo as he vowed to track down and do the same to the people that had taken them from him.

* * *

All three beauties continued to drink and joke while getting themselves ready to go out on the stage dressed in the skimpy exotic lingerie. Five strong shots later and they were all buzzed, and they then confidently stormed the dance floor. Nyte had them add twin stripper poles for the night; but after seeing the way the crowd was reacting to them, she planned on leaving the poles up if it was okay with Beysik.

Once on the makeshift stage, Aurora shed her self-consciousness by moving her hips deliciously to the beat of the loud music. The pounding bass made it easier for her to block out the lustful stares of the horny audience. Heaven had to admit to herself that she kind of missed the feeling of power as she swayed and seductively gyrated her way over to one of the poles. Heaven got right to showing off her skills.

Nyte did the same by moving over to Aurora, pulling her close and grinding on her to get her to focus on her instead of the eyes of the crowd surrounding them.

With the two of them dancing together and Heaven showing her talents high up on the pole behind them, the whole stage oozed sexiness. Heaven's thick legs caressed the polished brass while she continuously swirled her ass for the men standing on the sideline that were sprinkling her with cash. Aurora surprised them all when she dropped into a split, pulling Nyte down on top of her. The show that Aurora was trying to give was a little more than Nyte wanted to give them, so she seductively crawled away from her then pulled Aurora back up on her feet.

By the end of the Lil' Jon party mix, Aurora no longer looked at the stripper profession the same way. She now thought it was just fascinating. She stood in the middle of the cash littered dance floor assimilating the applause and power of her sex. The catcalls being screamed at her made her juices begin to flow, while Nyte and Heaven went around scooping up the cash that had been tossed their way.

When they returned to the dressing room and counted the cash, it totaled to over $1,300.

Aurora was dazzled by all of it. She now understood why so many young women chose the pole life. Nyte and Heaven decided that the drunk woman had had enough of their world and called it a night for her. A short time later, the trio rejoined the party fully dressed. They briefly hooked up with Beysik and the crew before Nyte broke away to take Aurora home. Heaven stayed behind to make sure the club got locked up properly. As Nyte drove Aurora's car to take her home, they talked and fondled a bit, but neither one of them noticed the Buick following closely behind them.

TWENTY - THREE

TABITHA SPENT A WEEK at her parents' home up in northern Wisconsin, and with all of the fresh air and free time on her hands, the busy minded detective had more time to think more clearly. Being at home made Tabitha think of Beysik. She just could not get the Bondz family to leave her thoughts. She felt the need to revisit the crime scene in person, because Tabitha felt like she had missed something that she was not seeing by only viewing the photos in the case file. She knew if Sadd had not been so gung-ho on putting Beysik Bondz behind bars, and really put in the effort to help her out with the Bondz family's murder case, she would have been able to enjoy her medical leave a whole lot better.

As Tabitha drove back down to Milwaukee, she continued her mental walkthrough of what she knew about the case so far, which was not much. All her hopes at this time were on the partial fingerprints that were pulled off of one of the spent shell casings that were found at the scene. So far they had not had any hits on the print that would give the detective the identity of the shooter.

Tabitha exited the interstate and headed straight to the scene of the crime. She did not have anyplace specific she wanted to check out again. She just needed to see it all. When she parked out front of the murder victims' home and got out, she noticed that it was now vacant with a large for sale sign stuck in the front lawn. Tabitha shook off her memory of the tragic night when her former partner shot the unarmed son of the victims, and in return was beaten half to death by the brother of his gunshot victim only minutes later.

Tabitha took a slow stroll down the block with her head on a constant swivel. The detective was scrutinizing every home and yard she passed, until she found something she had missed before. Right there was a camera system on a home across the street from where she stood, with the cameras pointing up and down the block. The house was located in the direction she had been told the gunmen had run in after the dirty deed. She crossed the street in a slow jog because her ribs were still a little sore. She was excited to interview the owner of the system, so she powered through it. As she got closer, she noticed an elderly woman on the side of the home trimming bushes.

"Excuse me, ma'am?" Tabitha interrupted her busy work. "Do you live here?" Tabitha asked, flashing the woman the shield she kept with her at all times out of habit.

"Yes I do, Detective," she confirmed, lowering the sharp hedge trimmer to her side and putting on a smile. "Is anything wrong?"

"No, ma'am, I'm hoping you can help me with something," she told her, getting right to what she needed from her. "I'm doing a follow-up investigation of the homicide that took place up the block from here."

"I'm familiar with it, but I did not know those people very well, and I was good and asleep when the shooting happened. So if you're looking to question me about it, I am sorry. But I didn't see anything."

"I understand that you did not, but what about your system there? Did you have it at the time of the shooting, or is it new?"

The old woman looked up at the cameras on her house as if she had forgotten they were up there. Then she smiled big.

"I've had them up a few years now. I had them put up to catch the son of a bitch who was

stealing my Sunday newspapers," she explained.

"Ma'am, I'm going to need to see the
recording of the night of the 18th, please."

"Oh sure, Detective. That's not a problem. I
keep them all just in case the rascal comes back
to steal something else," she told her as she
went inside the house for a few minutes. When
she returned, she had two DVDs in her hand.
"There's thirty-six hours on each of these. I
watch a lot of cop shows, so I figured you may
want to review the days before and after too,"
she explained as she handed over the disks.

Tabitha thanked her and then hurried back
to her car. She rushed home to watch the
recordings. When she pulled up to her house,
she saw Aurora's car parked on the street
instead of the driveway where it usually was at
this time of day. Tabitha did not think much of it.
Instead, her mind was on getting in the house
so she could view the DVDs hour by hour in
hopes of catching a killer or two.

"Aurrroora, I'm back!" she sang to the empty
house.

She did a quick walkthrough and guessed
her friend had gone out the night before and had
not made it in yet. Tabitha came up with that

from the various outfits that were still laid out on the bed. So she sent Aurora a text to let her know she was home early. She then put the first disk into the Blu-ray player and settled down in front of the TV to watch the videos.

Tabitha fast forwarded through the day to just before the estimated time of the murders. The old woman's home system caught the Bondzes' SUV pulling up and parking in front of their home. She made a note that the SUV was parked right where it was the night she was called to the scene. It also showed a dark fourdoor sedan pull over and park up the street from them closer to the camera. Two men got out and casually headed toward the unsuspecting couple still seated in the Escalade. The men split up as they closed in on the SUV, with one taking each side. Then one of them smashed the window, and a few seconds later the shooting started. When it was over, the men jogged back to the car with their guns in hand. Both men wore hoodies. One of them never showed his face, but the other looked right at the camera unknowingly before getting back into the car and speeding away. Tabitha replayed the fuzzy black and white video over and over, but she was only able to make out that the car was a Buick.

* * *

Aurora was the first to regain consciousness in the dark, unfamiliar room. She was shivering and scared, and her head was pounding. She could not see through the dark, but she knew she was not alone, because she could hear the sound of someone's labored breathing. She contemplated if she should say something or not, and then she remembered that Nyte was with her when she was last in her car.

Aurora strained her brain to remember what had happened after she had given Nyte her keys to drive her home, because she had too much to drink. She remembered them parking in front of Tabitha's house, and then suddenly being whacked in the face a few times by someone who had snatched her car door open. Then nothing!

"Hellooo! Hey, Nyte. Nyte, is that you? Please answer me. Wake up and answer me!" she pleaded, with her voice full of panic and desperation. When she did not get a response, Aurora took a chance and began crawling across the filthy floor toward the sound in the dark. "Oh my God, Nyte. If you're in here, please say something."

"Aurora?" Nyte finally groaned. "Where are you?" she asked, with her head pounding as she tried her best to see in the dark, funky place.

"I'm here. I'm coming to you. Just keep talking," she answered, not knowing that Nyte was so close in front of her. Aurora touched Nyte's leg, and they both let out a surprised shriek.

"Aurora, keep it down!" Nyte scolded her, because Aurora had been much louder. Nyte reached out and grabbed her arm and guided Aurora beside her.

"Oh my God! Oh my God! What happened? Where are we?"

"I don't know. I think we got kidnapped!" Nyte speculated in a low voice. "Just keep it down and try not to panic," she instructed while trying her best not to let her own terror make things worse.

Once Aurora was quiet, Nyte sat still and listened to try to hear anyone outside of the room, but she heard nothing.

"Oh my God! Oh my God!"

"Just breathe, Aurora. Panicking ain't gonna help us none!"

"Okay, okay, okay!" Aurora did her best to pull herself together. "My head is foggy and my jaw hurts like somebody beat me up. Nyte, this isn't your doing, is it, to show me how it was for you or to try to scare me?"

"What! Bitch, I'm in here with you! If I was gonna do some shit to scare you, it wouldn't be at my expense. I don't fuckin' believe you just said that stupid shit!"

"Please don't be mad. I'm sorry! It's just that I can't remember anything, and don't nobody got a reason to take me. Nyte, I'm sorry!" she begged for her forgiveness, squeezing Nyte's hand tightly so she could not pull it away from her again. "Nyte, do you remember anything?"

"I can see why you can think that this was me. It's okay, but, Aurora, you need to believe me and trust me when I tell you that this is real. Not me or anybody I know would do this to us. So I'm asking, do you trust me?"

"Yes," she answered weakly.

"Okay. My head hurts too. All I can remember is you trying to fight and him knocking us out in front of your house. I remember waking up from being pulled out of a car. I think we're in a junkyard or something," Nyte told her.

Nyte remembered the feeling of the unknown man's hands on her, and how he roughly held her around the waist as he dragged her limp body from the car. Nyte guessed that he was not a very big man because he kept dropping her. He had let her hit the ground several times before she got up the strength to attempt to fight. She remembered being hit with something hard like a gun before he slapped her and covered her face with a rag. There was nothing after that, until she woke up to the sound of Aurora's voice.

"How long do you think we've been here?"

"I don't know, but you gotta keep it together and help me think of a way outta here," she answered, trying to calm down her sobbing friend.

"What do you think he wants with us?"

As soon as the question left her lips, she thought of the FBI file and had to fight harder not to panic.

TWENTY - FOUR

OBLIVIOUS TO NYTE'S WHEREABOUTS or if she even had returned home the night before, Beysik sat finishing up an early lunch request from Asad at Starbucks along Miller Parkway. But at the last minute, Asad dropped out of the meeting but sent his business partner, Sky, in his place. Sky pitched a deal Beysik's way about using his girls to transport generic medications from Canada. This was Sky's side hustle. She explained to him that there was good money to be made by making the most common meds more affordable. Beysik listened, but all he wanted from her was bricks of cocaine at highway prices right there in the city.

"I'm only talking about two or maybe three girls that you feel are expendable," she said as they discussed business over large cappuccinos. "I will need more, but just not for our first go round. You know, just keep it simple."

Beysik thought Sky's ego was astounding. He really wanted to know what made her think he was some simple minded dude who would jeopardize his father's big money business for her petty side project. He thought she might just be on to something that Nyte could handle for him, but he was not going to tell Sky that.

"I'm not going to say no to what you're saying. I'm a businessman, so I'm always open to anything to do with making my pockets fatter, but I don't look at none of my team as expendable. Even an old one legged hag has her value," he said, quoting the late, great Mercy Bondz. "But I know a young up and coming pimp who has yet to learn the meaning of worth, that I could have holla at you and make this work out for the both of us," he suggested.

"If I never have to see him face to face, we have ourselves a deal," she replied, not used to not having a man slobbering to give her what she wanted from him by now.

"It sounds like a plan to me. Now about what I'm on. How do we do this? Do I prepay or POD?" He then flashed her a confident smile.

Beysik paid for Sky's refill to go after she agreed that they should pay on delivery for the first few times, just to get to know one another better. As he escorted her out to her car, he once again thought of something his father once told him. Mercy Bondz had told him that if he could make a person believe that they could not live without him, then they would do all of the pimping for him.

When Beysik got into his car, he checked his phones and wondered why he had not heard from Nyte by now. He also saw that it was almost time for his physical therapy, so he sent Nyte a text saying good morning and that he was on his way to his appointment. Beysik guessed she and Heaven were too busy working on the center's remodel to stop and call, because Heaven had not called him either.

* * *

Nyte was not going to allow the mental torture of being in the dark room paralyze her. She told Aurora to get up and help her try to find a light switch. After the two of them slowly inched their way around the room, heading in opposite directions, Nyte had a better understanding of the space they were in. The light switch panel Aurora found did not work, and the door beside it was locked tightly. Nyte wandered in the dark, sliding her hands along the brick wall until she came to a board. She instantly traced her hands around it and guessed from its shape and size that it had to be covering a window.

Her speculation was confirmed when she moved and found an identical board just a foot or so away. After trying to remove it with her bare hands with no luck, Nyte reunited with Aurora and sat back down on the floor.

"Tabi's up North visiting her parents, so nobody is looking for me. No one's looking!" Aurora cried out in defeat.

"That's not true! Someone's looking. Beysik is looking for me, so that means he's looking for us!"

"What makes you so sure? What, Nyte! Beysik is just another coldhearted pimp. This could be his doing, for all we know."

"No, bitch! I know better!" Nyte retorted. "He's not his father. He loves me; and when I did not come home, he called Heaven to see if I was with her and just lost my phone or something. After that, they, Beysik, Heaven, and his whole clique of goons, have been out searching for me. And you know what, Aurora? My man ain't gonna stop looking until he finds me," she stated, believing every word.

But she also understood that Beysik did not know where to start looking; and for that fact, she needed to find a way to get him a message. She dropped back against the wall and thought of ways to make that happen.

TWENTY - FIVE

WEEKENDS WERE THE ONLY days that the prison's meat department had only one meat man on duty. Noeekwol's off days were Saturdays, and House's were Sundays, because he liked to sit and enjoy the games during football season. Noeekwol did not mind it because Sundays were usually pretty easy compared to the rest of the week.

The champ was just finishing slicing up 6,400 pieces of turkey ham for the lunch meal the following day, when one of the kitchen supervisors rushed over and asked him to pull another fourteen cases of frozen mixed vegetables for that day's dinner meal. He told him that one of the cooks accidentally dumped the vegetables that were cooking.

"I can't believe Sutton dumped the kettle without checking it first this close to the meal."

"It's alright. I got it. It's a good thing it was just veggies and not the meat, or we might have had to eat these cold cuts for dinner tonight instead of tomorrow," Noeekwol joked with the supervisor about the inmate cook's mishap. He then finished panning up the turkey before he got to refilling the order.

* * *

Heaven was so busy with the carpenters and painting that by the time she realized that Nyte had not shown her face to help, it was 4:00 p.m.

"Fuck! Fuck! Fuck!" she swore to herself, because she had forgotten to add money on the phone to talk to Noeekwol. So she took a break and went out to her car to get her purse, so she could get the account replenished for the phone.

"What up, ma?"

Heaven looked up from her phone's screen to see who was speaking to her.

"Oh, hey!" she greeted Diesel.

"I see you out here doing your thang and exercising your boss bitch status."

"Yeah, a bitch can't shake her ass for cash forever."

"Hell, from what I seen at the spot the other night, you got a long way to go before you gotta give up your pole days. Y'all did y'all thang up there. I got that shit on video," he told her with a grin.

"Oh, do you?"

"Yep. You wanna see it?" he asked, still hanging out of the window of his coffee brown Dodge Durango LTD with matching wood grain and chrome 28 inch rims.

"Yeah, send it to me, please?" she said, casually raking pink strands of hair from her face.

"Hell yeah, I got you. Just give me your number."

"You got it already, or did you toss it out now that Bey is back?"

"Nawl! I just didn't know that was the same one you wanted me to send it to. You's a boss, and bosses usually got two phones. One for the plug and one for the hoes," he responded as he sent her the video.

"Hey, D, what are you doing up this way anyways?"

"My OG lives up here on 104th. I'm on my way to drop off some bread to her, so she and my daughters can go get their hair done," he answered proudly. "As a matter of fact, I gotta roll, so I'll catch you later."

Heaven waved and Diesel sped off, with his two 18 inch power bass subwoofers banging down the block. Heaven shook her head and made a mental note to put up a sign that read

No Loud Music when she got the place opened up. She then tried calling Nyte's phone before going back inside to finish up the wall she had been working on.

* * *

The girls did their best to pull themselves back together. Both of them were determined not to allow their fright to cease their will to fight any longer than it had already.

"A few years back, Mercy Bondz brought in this young girl from Syria, or maybe her name was Syria and she was from Tanzania. I don't remember right now, but—!"

"Wait, you said maybe her name was. What happened to her?" Aurora interrupted while clutching Nyte's hand tighter.

"That don't matter."

"But it does to me. What happened to her? I need to know, Nyte, please?"

Nyte closed her eyes and took a few breaths before she spoke again. She then explained how the girl went out on a date with a regular repeat caller who ended up beating her to death.

"Oh my God! Nooo! What happened to the man?"

"I don't know. All I know is that Mercy Bondz took care of it on both sides by giving Syria a real funeral. Yep, after the city cremated her, Pops claimed the ashes and buried her in a flower bed," Nyte explained, letting fresh tears slide down her cheeks. "Anyway, she taught me this prayer when I first met her. She said her mother made her learn it before she was sold to the militants in her village. I want you to say it with me now."

"Okay, I will," Aurora agreed in a shaky voice.

Oh God, You are the Author of peace, and from You comes peace. Blessed are You. Oh Lord of Majesty and Honor. Our God, please forgive me and my parents and my teachers and all the believing men and women. Give us your mercy. Oh most Merciful of all who show mercy. Amen!

When they finished the prayer, they hugged each other, got to their feet, and went in search of something they could use to pry the boards off of the windows or use to fight with, when whoever had taken them would return.

With nothing on the floor, Nyte went over to the corner where she had felt a set of thin pipes that ran up the wall during her search for the light switch. Both pipes were cool to the touch, so she did not know what ran through them. It could be water, which they both could use a drink of, or it could be gas, which would mean they had to work fast to get the board off the window before it killed them.

With no other choice, Nyte kicked at the conduit until it sprang free from the wall, just far enough for them to get a good grip on it with both hands. Nyte put her foot against the wall and pulled with all her might. The pipe bent more and more, but nothing happened, so Aurora took over and gave Nyte a break. This time, they were sprayed with cool water after it moved. Nyte instantly sprang back to her feet and helped Aurora break the conduit free. When it gave way, they were drenched with water. They both drank the water without a second thought, while laughing and crying with hopefulness.

TWENTY - SIX

TABITHA SAT IN HER home office going through the video of the Bondz murder on her desktop computer. She was unable to clear up the shot of the suspect's face, but she did, however, get a better view of the Buick's plate number. The detective was so excited about her work on the video that she decided to take advantage of her empty home. She skipped through the house into the bedroom, stripped off her clothes, climbed into bed, and stretched out on top of the covers.

Tabitha let her mind wander to the video. She visualized arresting the two killers and then delivering the good news to Beysik Bondz. As she thought about the handsome hoodlum, she got hornier. Tabitha fondled her breast with one hand while reaching into the drawer of the bedside table and retrieving her little pleasure toy, instantly turning it on. Just the feel of the pulsating clitoral stimulating device in her hand made her passion swell, and her juices began to flow.

Tabitha easily slipped back into her fantasy of Beysik rewarding her for a job well done. When he kissed her, she sucked on her own lip lustfully. She reached down between her knees and pressed the toy against her shaved mound. Then she slowly moved it to her clit so its vibrations could ease her longing itch. Beysik slammed her against the wall. Tabitha whimpered while working the toy around and around. She pictured the thug pushing her to her knees, where his big black erection was deliciously forced into her mouth. As she sucked, Aurora's ringtone began playing on her phone in the other room. It briefly interrupted her fantasy, but Tabitha was too caught up and too close with her self-pleasure to answer it, so she let the voicemail get it.

She added pressure to her clit and increased the speed, parting her creamy legs farther, opening herself to him more and more. When her legs started trembling, Tabitha dragged the toy through her wetness, imagining Beysik's head between her thighs. As the toy filled her opening, she moaned louder and louder until she screamed at her powerful, much needed release.

* * *

Beysik ambled into his place after being beat down from the workout that his bull like physical therapist pushed him through. He was so tired and sore that he dropped right down on the plush, soft leather sofa for a moment. The next thing he knew, he was being dragged awake by the ringing of his phone. Beysik did not realize that he had fallen asleep or that so much time had passed when he glanced at the time on the computer monitor.

Beysik wanted to go back to sleep, but the constant ringing of the phone's generic ringtone would not allow him to. It stopped and then started up again. Still a bit disoriented, he suddenly remembered that his brother could be calling from prison, which would explain the generic tone and the back to back calling.

"Yeah, hello?" he growled into the phone once he found the right one of the three on the coffee table. He tapped it to answer without looking at the number.

"Say, fam. If you want to see your bitches alive again, you need to bring me thirty Gs for each!" an unfamiliar male voice said.

"My bitches? Who is this? What bitches are you talking about?" Beysik questioned before he changed his mind. "Fuck that shit! You got' em, keep 'em!" he told the caller and then promptly ended the call.

He stared at the blocked number on the screen and wondered who was playing on his phone. He then remembered that he had not heard from Nyte or Heaven yet that day. Beysik was about to call Nyte's phone when the blocked number called back.

"Who the fuck is this?" he demanded.

"Beysik Bondz, son of Mercy Bondz. That was just so fuckin' rude of you and plain careless. Now if I was taking a play out of the Mercy Bondz's playbook, a bitch would be dying right about now. But I know you truly didn't mean what you said about letting me have these bitches. Well, maybe the one, but not this sexy black ass bitch. No, no! She's your personal."

Right then Beysik knew that the caller was talking about Nyte, so he had to think of something quick.

"All my bitches are personal to me, so you're going to have to do better than that, homie!" Beysik said, trying to keep him on the line while he called Nyte's phone on one of his other lines.

"Now do you really want to play this game? Do you want to bet your girl's toes on this game?

Do you really wanna find out that way if I'm joking or not?"

For a few long moments, Beysik's mind froze. He knew that Nyte had not come home, because she would have awakened him to eat or to get in the bed and off of the couch. When he remembered to breathe again, he got up and rushed through the house looking for any sign that she had been there since he left that morning, while asking the caller for proof of life.

"How do I know you won't be sending me a few already dead toes?" Beysik asked while trying to remain as calm as he could. "I want to talk to both of them so I'm sure they're alive."

"I understand, but you don't make demands, I do. So if you don't want me to play with my shiny new blade, it's best you answer when I call back. If you make me wait like before, I'm going to start cutting. Now that was from your dear old daddy's playbook." He laughed and ended the call.

With that on his mind and a dead phone to his ear, all Beysik could think to do was call Heaven, since Nyte's phone had gone straight to voicemail. He needed to see if Heaven was alright, because he knew from Diesel that she had been working at the daycare earlier in the day. Beysik relaxed a bit when he heard her voice come across the line. Beysik was relieved that he did not have to worry about her life as well. He gave Heaven instructions to immediately carry out before ending the call and calling his squad.

* * *

Slim's demented laughter filled the air. He was feeling proud of how his plan was coming together. He would soon have his partner back, as well as all of the cash that Mercy Bondz had taken from his family and then some for his troubles. He never thought that it would be so easy to pull off on his own after he had come up with the idea to get Fame released. When Asad told Slim about the female detective who was overseeing Fame's case, from that moment on, Slim made it his business to keep tabs on her so he could find something to use to scheme her into doing what he needed done.

During his surveillance of detective Tabitha Allison, Slim had not once seen the lovely detective with a man or children, just a woman. But from watching their interactions with one another, he knew that relationship was just friendly, which was good enough for him. It was a bonus when Asad asked him to accompany him to the party at Members Only. That was where he saw the detective's friend, Aurora, dancing on stage with two other girls. It was then that he decided that it was the best time to put his plan into action. Slim told Asad that he should not go into business with Mercy Bondz's son because he did not believe that it was just a coincidence that Beysik's girl and the detective's friend were so close.

With that said, Slim broke away from the party and went out to his car. He followed Aurora and Nyte when they left the club an hour later. He took them as soon as the timing was right. He had not planned on taking Nyte; but since she was there, he felt he could get even more revenge for what the pimp had done to his little cousins.

TWENTY - SEVEN

COLD WATER FROM THE broken pipe relentlessly covered the floor and flowed beneath the door. Nyte and Aurora were determined to prevail through the living hell they were in. Nyte took the roughly twenty-two foot piece of conduit that she had snapped off of the water main and went over to the window. She needed to find out how thick the board covering it was, knowing the density of the wood would tell her how to attack it.

"Stand back!" she told Aurora as she ran and kicked the center of the board as hard as she could with her bare foot. The wood flexed and broke the glass that was put in place to protect it.

The sound of the shattered glass and cracked wood got their adrenaline rushing. This time Aurora kicked at it. She gave it three powerful kicks before her foot hurt, but her pain was not without reward. A thin beam of dull light seeped in from the bottom corner of the board.

"I broke it a little! You see it?" Aurora asked excitedly while touching the area.

"Stand back and let me see if I can make a hole big enough so I can get this pipe under it. Then we can pry it off and get the fuck outta here," Nyte told her. She then went to work digging at the wood with the sharpest end of the conduit. "I don't know what that muthafucka got in mind for us, but whatever it is, he picked the wrong two bitches to fuck with!" she exclaimed, chipping off a small chunk of wood.

* * *

Tabitha was fresh out of the shower, standing in the bathroom while blow drying her hair in the mirror, when she heard her best friend's set ringtone begin to play. This time she did not ignore it. Instead, she dropped what she was doing and rushed into her office to catch the call.

"Hey, girl, I'm sorry!"

"Detective, I'm not your girl, and I'm not trying to hear that shit!" Slim growled at her.

"Wait, who are you, and why do you have my friend's phone?" she demanded after her apology was so rudely interrupted by the unknown man on the phone.

"Who I am is unimportant. All you need to worry about is what I will do if you don't do what the fuck I say, Detective T. Allison!" Slim paused, making her name sound more threatening than the words he was using. "I have your pretty friend here alive and well. But if you want her to remain that way, you will choose your next move wisely."

"Let me speak to Aurora now or I'm hanging up!"

"Do not hang up this phone! I'll hurt her if you do!" he retorted.

"You know, your CI hung up on me, and I didn't like it. I'm going to tell you the same shit I told him. If you test me in any way, I'm going to start cutting off bits and pieces of these bitches for you to find when I'm done!" He chuckled like a psychopath.

"What do you want?" Tabitha asked, pacing the floor, nude from her shower.

"I want you to drop that Michigan Street massacre case that you are trying to pin on my friend. You know, the one who you have under guard at the hospital."

"I can't do that," she retorted, knowing that he did not know that Fame had been moved to the county lockup's infirmary.

"You can and you will, Detective. This isn't up for negotiation. Your clock has started, and so have I, sharpening my knife. So drop the case and let him go."

"Before I try to do anything, I want proof of life. How do I know she is still alive?"

"I knew that was coming. She's very much alive, Detective. I am not a liar. I will let you talk to her in an hour. Just answer the phone. And please don't get your police buddies involved, or you can guess what I will do. Bye!"

The call promptly ended. Tabitha could not believe this was happening. She knew she was to blame for Aurora's life being in the hands of death. Right then she stopped pacing because the two suspects from the Bondzes' murder case popped into mind. Tabitha shook it off because there was no way the two were related, but it gave her an idea. She typed Aurora's phone number into the Friend Finder app on her phone, and within seconds she was rewarded with a map of Aurora's phone's current location.

"Thank God for stupid criminals," she said, rushing to get dressed so she could use the app's GPS to find Aurora instead of waiting on the psycho to call her back.

The detective reviewed Aurora's travel history, and she guessed that the reason the caller did not put her on the phone was that he was not around her actual location. So Tabitha planned to retrace its movements to the best place the phone was last at and save Aurora without him knowing. She would then find him and end this for good.

Tabitha knew that what she was about to do was wrong and went against her training and better judgment, but she had to go save her friend alone. She had to go try to save Aurora, who might not even be her friend anymore after this was over. As she dressed, she pondered how someone could forgive someone after being kidnapped because of her. When she was done and all strapped up, she rushed out to her car. But she wondered who the CI was that the caller had mentioned he had spoken to.

* * *

Standing in almost ankle deep water and dripping in sweat, Nyte took a short break from chopping at the board while Aurora had her ear pressed to the door listening for footsteps coming to investigate all of the banging they were doing. After the break, Nyte went right back to work and was soon able to peel off a large piece of wood, which left a hole only big enough for their heads to fit through. It brought more light into the room, which also boosted their adrenaline. The silhouettes had a brief, joyful embrace, and then they both reached in and pulled at the opening.

Just as the board started to give way, they heard someone cussing about the water and them messing with the door. They readied themselves for the fight they were about to put up to get out of the room. Nyte and Aurora stood on either side of the door, hoping to catch them by surprise. They both noticed that there was still only one voice on the outside. Nyte liked their odds with the two of them against the one of him.

The locks on the other side of the door clicked, and as soon as the door opened wide enough for Slim to step through, Aurora rammed the door with her shoulder and slammed it back into him with all she had. Slim staggered back, dazed a bit, and before he knew what was happening, Nyte had commenced to murderously whacking him with the pipe. Slim dropped to the floor howling in pain and surprise. In her rage, Nyte took the pointed end of the pipe and stabbed her assailant in the abdomen. She and Aurora then jetted off, running as fast as their sore, wet bare feet would allow them to. They dodged debris and ran through broken glass covering the floor, but they did not stop or slow up their escape.

TWENTY - EIGHT

TABITHA'S PHONE APP LED her to Members Only. She checked her friend's phone's current location to see that it had moved from the upper west side location that it was in twenty minutes ago when she left her home. Tabitha quickly got out of her car when she spotted Heaven approaching the side entrance of the building.

"You stop right there! Don't make me shoot you!" she bellowed with her gun trained at Heaven's chest.

"Detective Allison, I'm glad you're here," Heaven said, stopping to face her. "Somebody took Nyte and Aurora last night, and Beysik is out trying to find them," she explained.

Even though the time stamp of the location matched what she had just been told, the detective still had to be sure.

"Why was Aurora here with Nyte last night?"

"She just wanted to hang out with us, I guess. Why is that important? Call your police friends and go find them. And stop pointing your gun at me," Heaven answered, getting very animated.

"Okay, I believe you," Tabitha said as she lowered her gun but did not holster it. "I got a call from someone claiming to have them, so I traced Aurora's last known location to here."

"I can promise you that they are not here. You can come in and look for yourself. The only reason I'm here is that Beysik told me to meet him here so he can keep me safe until he finds them."

Just as Heaven was explaining, a fully custom 1971 Chevy Caprice pulled up behind Heaven's car. QXL and two more of Beysik's goons spilled out of it and hurried toward the two women.

"Are they with you?" Tabitha asked, seeing QXL with his Glock out.

She got ready to drop him and his buddies if she had to.

"Yeah!" Heaven answered before she told the men to stand down. "Beysik must have called them here. I told you he's getting ready to go kicking in doors looking for Nyte and Aurora."

"Hey, download the Friend Finder app onto your phone and put in my number. I believe I know where they are, but I need to go there right now. So when Beysik gets here, tell him to use the app to find me, because he's the only

ASSA RAYMOND BAKER

backup I can take without getting them killed by
the psycho that has them."

Once Tabitha was sure that Heaven was all
set up, she got back in her car and sped away
toward the current location of Aurora's phone.
She pushed the car past the posted speed limit
just enough not to flag one of her fellow law
enforcement officers, who she could not afford
to have pull her over. She raced down 27th
Street until the GPS told her to take a left turn
onto Clark Street. She slowed down upon
seeing that she was nearing the place where the
phone had stopped.

The app pointed her to the abandoned
Milwaukee Satellite warehouse. There in the
parking lot, she found a dark colored Buick just
like the one she had seen in the video, and she
could not believe it. But she knew that if it was
the same car from the video, the guy she had
talked to on the phone was indeed a killer, so
she did not have time to waste looking at it. She
parked helter skelter and blocked in the car with
hers. She then got out of her car with gun in
hand and tactfully approached the slightly ajar
loading dock entrance door.

Tabitha shifted her body to make herself less
of a noticeable target as she inched to the door.

She was only a few feet away from the door when she suddenly heard the sound of rushing feet. Just before she could get to the door, both Nyte and Aurora came rocketing out of the darkness right toward her.

* * *

Diesel drove while Beysik kept his eyes glued to the screen of Heaven's phone. He watched the little red flashing triangle that represented the detective. The two angrily zigzagged through the city's side streets, following the GPS to the heart of the notorious Murder Mob street gang's neighborhood. Beysik wondered if they were the ones who had taken his girl, and if so, why would they start this war with him for that little bit of cash?

Once they turned onto Clark Street, Beysik sat up straight, put down the phone, and picked up his gun. The friend tracker took them to the end of the block where Clark Street abruptly ended at the old warehouse. Diesel slowed down and crept up inside the parking lot of the place, where they found the detective and both girls standing in tears beside two cars. Beysik jumped out of the truck and rushed over to Nyte.

Nyte saw him and stood to meet him, but out of nowhere, Slim emerged from the darkness of the warehouse, immediately busting his gun at them. Nyte went down hard. Beysik, Tabitha, and Diesel instantly returned fire, killing the already dying hit man.

"Nyte, are you alright?" Beysik asked, limping over to her side.

"Yeah, I just fell," she informed him, with a bloody scrape on the right side of her face.

"You two have to give me your weapons and get outta here," Tabitha said to the men facing her. "Beysik, I gotta call this in, and you two can't be here when I do. It would be too hard to explain," she said, holding her hand out for Diesel's and Beysik's guns.

"Alright, here!" Beysik handed over his. "Nyte, let's go!"

"No, she has to stay."

"Why?" Beysik inquired while staring at the detective.

"Look at them. They're both covered in bruises and blood. My team will find their DNA inside and start looking for her if she's not here."

"It's okay, Bey. I trust her. Just go. I'ma call you as soon as I can get to a phone," Nyte said while sitting on the trunk of Tabitha's car to get off her feet.

"I'm going to need your gun too," Tabitha told Diesel.

"Nawl, I'm good. I don't know you like that," he retorted, gripping his weapon tighter at his side.

"Self, just give it to her and let's get the fuck outta here so she can clean this shit up!" Beysik ordered the thug.

Diesel reluctantly did as he was told, but not before he thoroughly wiped off the weapon with his shirt. He handed it over to the detective, and she thanked him before she retrieved her phone from her back pocket. She then made the call as soon as the two men were inside Diesel's SUV pulling away.

EPILOGUE

THE CHAMP FINISHED PUTTING the cold cut meat away, and then grabbed a cart and went inside the freezer to retrieve the boxes of veggies needed to replace the ones that were dumped. He was busily filling the cart when Flip and two more of his goons flooded into the cold space. They were all armed with curled, jagged prison blades. Noeekwol instantly turned to face the three hostiles and knew that he had been set up for an ambush.

Noeekwol tossed the 13 ¼ pound box at the men and promptly followed the distraction with an unsuspecting roundhouse kick to one of Flip's flunky's chest. The hard kick sent him flying backward, crashing into a ten foot tower of frozen broccoli. Several of the thirty pound boxes tumbled down on him. At that time, Flip and the other man stormed forward swinging their shanks. Noeekwol was slashed across his arm when he attempted to block Flip's strike, but then ended up getting slashed in the face by the other man. The two inch gash ran from the champ's left temple across the eye to his cheek.

The blade just missed the eye itself. Flip continued to press forward with his blade swinging more recklessly now that he saw blood.

Noeekwol pushed the cart of mixed vegetables out of the way, which blocked Flip from being able to attack him. The champ then timed the goon's strikes and caught the man's arm the next time he went to jab the shank at him. Holding on tight, Noeekwol spun his big body the opposite direction of the goon's elbow joint, breaking it. He then instantly commenced to murderously slamming reverse elbow strikes into the poor man's face. When Noeekwol released his hold on him, the goon fell limply onto the cold freezer floor.

With nobody between the two of them, Flip turned and fled from the freezer. This time, he used the cart to slow the champ to make his getaway. Noeekwol tumbled over the cart but quickly regained his footing and took off after Flip. When he burst from the freezer, which was a bloody mess, he ran right into Officer Buckley standing there. Flip was nowhere in sight.

"Bondz, what happened?"

Noeekwol paused a minute before answering. He then turned to face the officer.

"We fell trying to get the boxes," he said, allowing Buckley to escort him across to HSU to get patched up, vowing to himself to get even with Flip.

* * *

At approximately 9:45 a.m., Detective Allison sat across from her commanding officer debriefing on her night's events. She explained how Slim had contacted her in an attempt to blackmail her into copping her case on Fame. She admitted to using the app to locate the hostages; and at that time, she discovered that the man now deceased was also involved in two of her open cases. Tabitha concluded her debriefing by telling him that when the suspect fired on her, she returned fire, killed him, and saved the women. When questioned about the other two guns, she stated that she took them from the suspect's car when she cleared it to make sure no one else was hiding inside.

To order books, please fill out the order form below:
To order films please go to www.good2gofilms.com

Name:_____

Address:_____

City:_____State:_____Zip Code: _____

Phone:_____

Email:_____

Method of Payment: Check   VISA MASTERCARD

Credit Card#:_ _____

Name as it appears on card: _____

Signature: _____

Item Name	Price	Qty	Amount
48 Hours to Die – Silk White	$14.99		
A Hustler's Dream – Ernest Morris	$14.99		
A Hustler's Dream 2 – Ernest Morris	$14.99		
A Thug's Devotion – J. L. Rose and J. M. McMillon	$14.99		
All Eyes on Tommy Gunz – Warren Holloway	$14.99		
Black Reign – Ernest Morris	$14.99		
Bloody Mayhem Down South – Trayvon Jackson	$14.99		
Bloody Mayhem Down South 2 – Trayvon Jackson	$14.99		
Business Is Business – Silk White	$14.99		
Business Is Business 2 – Silk White	$14.99		
Business Is Business 3 – Silk White	$14.99		
Cash In Cash Out – Assa Raymond Baker	$14.99		
Cash In Cash Out 2 – Assa Raymond Baker	$14.99		
Childhood Sweethearts – Jacob Spears	$14.99		
Childhood Sweethearts 2 – Jacob Spears	$14.99		
Childhood Sweethearts 3 – Jacob Spears	$14.99		
Childhood Sweethearts 4 – Jacob Spears	$14.99		
Connected To The Plug – Dwan Marquis Williams	$14.99		
Connected To The Plug 2 – Dwan Marquis Williams	$14.99		
Connected To The Plug 3 – Dwan Williams	$14.99		
Cost of Betrayal – W.C. Holloway	$14.99		
Cost of Betrayal 2 – W.C. Holloway	$14.99		
Deadly Reunion – Ernest Morris	$14.99		
Dream's Life – Assa Raymond Baker	$14.99		
Flipping Numbers – Ernest Morris	$14.99		

Flipping Numbers 2 – Ernest Morris	$14.99		
He Loves Me, He Loves You Not – Mychea	$14.99		
He Loves Me, He Loves You Not 2 – Mychea	$14.99		
He Loves Me, He Loves You Not 3 – Mychea	$14.99		
He Loves Me, He Loves You Not 4 – Mychea	$14.99		
He Loves Me, He Loves You Not 5 – Mychea	$14.99		
Killing Signs – Ernest Morris	$14.99		
Killing Signs 2 – Ernest Morris	$14.99		
Kings of the Block – Dwan Willams	$14.99		
Kings of the Block 2 – Dwan Willams	$14.99		
Lord of My Land – Jay Morrison	$14.99		
Lost and Turned Out – Ernest Morris	$14.99		
Love & Dedication – W.C. Holloway	$14.99		
Love Hates Violence – De'Wayne Maris	$14.99		
Love Hates Violence 2 – De'Wayne Maris	$14.99		
Love Hates Violence 3 – De'Wayne Maris	$14.99		
Love Hates Violence 4 – De'Wayne Maris	$14.99		
Married To Da Streets – Silk White	$14.99		
M.E.R.C. – Make Every Rep Count Health and Fitness	$14.99		
Mercenary In Love – J.L. Rose & J.L. Turner	$14.99		
Money Make Me Cum – Ernest Morris	$14.99		
My Besties – Asia Hill	$14.99		
My Besties 2 – Asia Hill	$14.99		
My Besties 3 – Asia Hill	$14.99		
My Besties 4 – Asia Hill	$14.99		
My Boyfriend's Wife – Mychea	$14.99		
My Boyfriend's Wife 2 – Mychea	$14.99		
My Brothers Envy – J. L. Rose	$14.99		
My Brothers Envy 2 – J. L. Rose	$14.99		
Naughty Housewives – Ernest Morris	$14.99		
Naughty Housewives 2 – Ernest Morris	$14.99		
Naughty Housewives 3 – Ernest Morris	$14.99		
Naughty Housewives 4 – Ernest Morris	$14.99		
Never Be The Same – Silk White	$14.99		
Scarred Knuckles – Assa Raymond Baker	$14.99		

Scarred Knuckles 2 – Assa Raymond Baker	$14.99		
Shades of Revenge – Assa Raymond Baker	$14.99		
Slumped – Jason Brent	$14.99		
Someone's Gonna Get It – Mychea	$14.99		
Stranded – Silk White	$14.99		
Supreme & Justice – Ernest Morris	$14.99		
Supreme & Justice 2 – Ernest Morris	$14.99		
Supreme & Justice 3 – Ernest Morris	$14.99		
Tears of a Hustler – Silk White	$14.99		
Tears of a Hustler 2 – Silk White	$14.99		
Tears of a Hustler 3 – Silk White	$14.99		
Tears of a Hustler 4 – Silk White	$14.99		
Tears of a Hustler 5 – Silk White	$14.99		
Tears of a Hustler 6 – Silk White	$14.99		
The Last Love Letter – Warren Holloway	$14.99		
The Last Love Letter 2 – Warren Holloway	$14.99		
The Panty Ripper – Reality Way	$14.99		
The Panty Ripper 3 – Reality Way	$14.99		
The Solution – Jay Morrison	$14.99		
The Teflon Queen – Silk White	$14.99		
The Teflon Queen 2 – Silk White	$14.99		
The Teflon Queen 3 – Silk White	$14.99		
The Teflon Queen 4 – Silk White	$14.99		
The Teflon Queen 5 – Silk White	$14.99		
The Teflon Queen 6 – Silk White	$14.99		
The Vacation – Silk White	$14.99		
Tied To A Boss – J.L. Rose	$14.99		
Tied To A Boss 2 – J.L. Rose	$14.99		
Tied To A Boss 3 – J.L. Rose	$14.99		
Tied To A Boss 4 – J.L. Rose	$14.99		
Tied To A Boss 5 – J.L. Rose	$14.99		
Time Is Money – Silk White	$14.99		
Tomorrow's Not Promised – Robert Torres	$14.99		
Tomorrow's Not Promised 2 – Robert Torres	$14.99		
Two Mask One Heart – Jacob Spears and Trayvon Jackson	$14.99		
Two Mask One Heart 2 – Jacob Spears and Trayvon Jackson	$14.99		

Two Mask One Heart 3 – Jacob Spears and Trayvon Jackson	$14.99		
Wrong Place Wrong Time – Silk White	$14.99		
Young Goonz – Reality Way	$14.99		
Subtotal:			
Tax:			
Shipping (Free) U.S. Media Mail:			
Total:			

Make Checks Payable To: Good2Go Publishing, 7311 W Glass Lane, Laveen, AZ 85339

CPSIA information can be obtained
at www.ICGtesting.com
Printed in the USA
LVHW011603020720
659594LV00009B/1107